HARMONY HOUSE

NIC SHEFF

HARPER TEEN
An Imprint of HarperCollinsPublishers

HarperTeen is an imprint of HarperCollins Publishers.

Harmony House
Copyright © 2016 by Nic Sheff
All rights reserved. Printed in the United States of America.
No part of this book may be used or reproduced in any manner
whatsoever without written permission except in the case of brief
quotations embodied in critical articles and reviews.
For information address HarperCollins Children's Books,
a division of HarperCollins Publishers, 195 Broadway, New York, NY 10007.
www.epicreads.com

ISBN 978-0-06-233709-2 (trade bdg.)

Typography by Sarah Nichole Kaufman
16 17 18 19 20   CG/RRDH   10 9 8 7 6 5 4 3 2 1
❖
First Edition

To Bert V. Royal and Karen DiConcetto . . .
for being the most incredible, kind, brilliant people I know.
I admire you both very much.

HARMONY HOUSE
November 1867

Cornelia Baron
17 years old

PROLOGUE

There's a feeling like my stomach is trying to climb out my throat. I drop on my hands and knees in the tall grass and retch. The sun is hot and bright overhead, so I'm sweating through my clothes. I take off the heavy topcoat and unbutton the shirt around my neck.

A pain cuts in along my thigh and I pull up my petticoat and see the vibrant shock of red turning dark and sticky along the white of my skin. I must have fallen on a sharp rock in the grass. There's a purplish bruise already forming there.

I spit on the cut and rub it with my thumb.

I stand.

A snake, black and glinting in the sun, slithers past.

I jump back and start to cross myself.

But it's too late.

I let my arm drop.

From the branches of the low-hanging willow tree a kestrel falcon darts out into the clear morning—its markings black, painted around its eyes like a bandit. The bird flies high up over the field and I watch it silhouetted against the yellow-orange sun. It dives down in a flash and grabs a small wood rat from out of the dandelion. The rat screams a terrible, piercing scream as the falcon's claws dig in and it is carried off over the dense forest.

My cat, Jonas, comes running from under the white-painted front porch at the sound of the wounded animal. He scans the yard, but sees nothing.

From inside I hear my mother calling.

Her voice carries through the still air.

She calls my name. Again and again.

"Cornelia? Cornelia Barron?"

The windows are pushed up all around the house because of the warm weather and I can hear her getting closer.

I grab my coat off the ground and limp back behind a line of white-blossoming cottonwood trees.

My breath feels sharp in my lungs and I taste blood, like tin, at the back of my throat.

Mother steps out onto the porch, calling my name again. Her long hair is pitch-dark, curled, and tied with ribbon. She wears a crimson dress, bound tight around her waist. Mother and father are taking the kit and buggy into market this morning. I can't face seeing her again—not now. I've already said good-bye.

So I ignore her calls and slip away down the worn deer trail through the tangled blackberry and poison ivy and pale beech trees with the bark peeling white. Her voice fades behind me and soon I am out in a field of sweet-smelling lavender and sunflowers grown up taller even than I am. The pain in my leg is gone and I run fast—trying to get clear of the house and the sickness and my mother and father and this sin growing here, inside of me.

I run until I cross the wide dirt road and then I double over sick again. I vomit and taste more blood, but my stomach is empty, so only a little yellowish liquid comes up.

I am very thirsty now.

I have no choice but to cut down through the woods

to where the stream pools in an almost perfect circle of brackish water and mossy rocks. The cut over my knee opens up and I can feel the warm blood drip down my leg as I drink the water from my cupped hands.

The taste is nauseating.

Everything seems to be.

The demon has taken hold of me.

It lived dormant all these years—waiting—biding its time—until I was weak enough. Then it came upon me in my sleep, crawling spiderlike up the outside wall and coming in through my open window. It lay with me. It drank my blood. It covered me with its damp, rough body. It kissed me so my face was red and swollen. Its breath was hot and stank of whiskey. It drove itself into me. And it left this curse behind. The curse that swells my belly and makes my bleeding stop and turns the world stinking and noxious.

The curse that damns my soul to burn in white-hot flames.

For all eternity.

There's no going back now. I deserve all the pain and the nausea and the swelling. I deserve more.

On the road above me I hear the jangling of the bridle and the creaking wheels and the heavy gait of my father's bay horse. Mother and father riding to town in the bouncing carriage. They travel fast and soon are out of hearing. I whisper good-bye to them one more time. I whisper good-bye to the big bay.

The demon takes my hand. I grab a fist of my hair, long and black like my mother's. I scream and pull down hard and fast so my scalp tears away in a bleeding mass of black hair and skin and black blood. The clump of scalp I've ripped away is only the size of a small gold piece, but it burns and bleeds steady.

I bury the hair in the damp clay earth beside the pool.

I spit and cross myself three times.

But there is no penance left.

The curse is too deep inside me.

I drink again and get slowly to my feet.

Jonas has followed me. He watches, crouched, from beneath the nettles. He is gray with long hair and golden eyes. I coax him out, making a clicking noise with my tongue on the roof of my mouth. He swishes his tail and arches his back. I pick him up and kiss the top of his head. He swishes his tail even more, though he doesn't run away.

We walk together through the darkening forest.

There is a wind now making a sound like the ocean in the trees. It seems to grow ever louder—the leaves and branches beginning to thrash wildly.

Dark clouds appear to cover the fading brilliance of the midday sun.

The dry field pops with blue flashes of electric currents like lightning across the yellowed grass.

The wind seems to come from all directions.

Jonas and I run to the barn door, the horses stamping and snorting restless inside, the goats bleating loudly.

The hay smell is sour and rotting and I can hear the rats squealing shrilly in the loft above us. Jonas goes off to hunt, unafraid of the storm. A barn owl, white-faced and green-eyed, peers out from the rafters.

I walk past the gray colt, Texas, and my mother's sorrel mare, both horses pacing back and forth, agitated, kicking at the floor. Lancer stands trembling in the last stall, while the black-and-white goat with the bowlegs takes refuge in the straw behind him.

A clap of thunder sounds all around us and I go to Lancer to try to calm him down. He's a tall horse, lean and sinewy—a painted Indian pony—with thick veins bulging up and down his neck and legs. His eyes roll white in his head and he stamps and trembles. I take his reins out from my coat pocket and loop them over his muzzle and whisper in his ear:

"It will be all right.

It will be all right.

It will be all right."

Even though that is a lie.

I gather the thick coil of rope from off the stall door and secure it firmly over my shoulder. I lay the saddle blanket across Lancer's heaving back and lead him out through the barn. Lancer bucks and rolls his eyes more, but I hold the reins tight.

Outside the wind is strong so the branches bend nearly to the ground. The sky is black now beneath the clouds.

I think then that if Lancer would only buck me off—or if I were to set him at a gallop and just let go—I could maybe break my leg or arm or back and lose this evil festering inside me.

But it wouldn't matter.

The evil here cannot be cut out—no matter how hard I try.

It is in me.

And there is no escape.

Tears burn in my eyes. I unhitch the bridle and feed Lancer a cube of sugar from my outstretched hand. I kiss him on his wet, lathering neck and hold him to me, whispering all the time in his ear.

I take the saddle blanket off and wrap it around my shivering body.

Another clap of thunder sounds.

Lancer rears up on his hind legs.

"Go," I tell him. "Go on."

He looks at me with his dark, bugging eyes.

"Go."

I strike him once firmly and then he understands.

He runs north, toward the river.

He is set free.

I turn and walk back to the house.

Rain falls like frozen sheets across the field.

I walk with my head down—crying hard so I can barely catch my breath.

The cold cuts into me.

I gasp and work my hands at the rope unconsciously as I walk.

I am soaked through and dripping wet by the time I reach the house. I climb the dark wood staircase to the third floor—leaving a trail of mud and my discarded clothing.

The rain against the stained glass windows and shingled roofs sounds like rocks falling.

There are paintings done in oils of Jesus among the

Romans and Lazarus risen from the dead. There is Jonah and the Whale and the Virgin Mary with Child and the Tower of Babel and Sodom and Gomorrah. There are silver crucifixes mounted on every door.

I keep myself from looking.

I cannot face my own failure to God, to His son, to my mother and father.

I have failed them all.

The rope itches rough around my throat as I tighten the noose.

Tears stream down my face.

My heart beats loudly in my ears.

There is nothing else for me now.

I climb up onto the banister.

My legs tremble.

I close my eyes.

A fire courses through my blood.

Fire that will consume my body for all eternity.

A fire hotter than the center of the earth and sun and planets colliding.

I breathe.

I breathe.

I step off the banister.

I fall.

HARMONY HOUSE

November 1997

Jennifer Noonan

CHAPTER 1

There's a feeling like my stomach is trying to climb out my throat. I choke the nausea down and breathe and try to block out the smell of grease and frying bacon. I take a sip of coffee and sit back in the corner of the torn vinyl booth.

Dad reads the paper, looking tired, with dark circles cut deep under both eyes. His hair has gone almost completely white in the past few months. There are lines set deep around his mouth and at the corners of his eyes—his eyes, which are almost transparent blue, gray and clouded. He's grown weak and pale.

The waitress, a haggard, aging blonde with her roots grown out dark, sets a plate of eggs and hash browns in front of my dad and a chocolate donut in front of me.

"Thank you," my dad tells her.

And I say, "Thanks."

She asks if we need anything else. My dad says no, thank you. She walks off to the next customer. She doesn't smile.

My dad puts his paper down and folds it neatly on the bench seat.

"We should be there before dark," he says.

I roll my eyes without really meaning to.

"Great."

"Come on, Jen," he tells me. "You've gotta try."

"I am," I say.

I tear off a piece of the greasy-feeling donut.

"Wait," my dad says, placing his hands on mine.

I put the donut back.

"Come on," he says. "You know better than that."

I take another sip of coffee.

"It's all you," I tell him.

He lays his palms down flat on the cracked linoleum table. He bows his head. His heavy eyelids flutter and close.

I glance around at the other customers in the dingy, smoke-filled diner. None of them seem to notice my father with his bowed head. Mostly they look like local farmers or long distance truckers. There's one mother with a little boy at a booth in the corner. Her jaw click-clicks back and forth. The boy looks very dirty.

"Our Father," my dad says, "Who art in Heaven, hallowed be thy name. Thy Kingdom come, thy Will be done, on Earth as it is in Heaven. Give us this day, our daily bread. And forgive us our trespasses, as we forgive those who trespass against us. And lead us not into temptation, but deliver us from evil. For thine is the kingdom, and the power, and the glory forever and ever. Amen. Thank you for this food, and God bless the soul of our Maggie. We miss her very much."

"*Dad,*" I say.

There are tears in his eyes.

"She's in a better place now," he says.

I tell him I don't doubt it.

He wipes the tears away with his long, knotted fingers.

"We can't be selfish, wanting her back with us," he says.

"But I *do*. I do want her back."

He shakes his head.

"It was God's will for her. And it was God's will for us."

"Then God's an asshole," I say.

He strikes fast across the table like a snake and smacks me in the mouth.

I hold my jaw and look around the restaurant again.

No one seems to have noticed.

The farmers and truck drivers stay hunched over their plates.

"You watch your mouth," he tells me.

"Cocksucker," I say, but not loud enough so he can hear.

"What's that?"

"Nothing," I tell him.

I eat the chocolate donut and drink the weak coffee.

"I've tried with you, Jen. I've tried and tried."

He breaks the bright orange, toxic-looking egg yolk so it goes dripping out over the ham and potatoes. He smears it around with his knife and takes in big mouthfuls as he talks. It's enough to make me sick.

"When are you going to learn?" he asks. "How many times do I have to tell you?"

I swallow the last of the coffee down and stand, pushing the table back toward my dad roughly.

"I've gotta go to the bathroom," I say.

I don't look at him.

The waitress comes over to ask if everything is all right.

I know what the answer is.

But I don't say it.

I walk on past her.

To get to the diner bathroom I have to walk outside and around to the back of the building. The sky is clear and cold, so I can see the steam of my breath in the early morning. Already the leaves on the trees have changed colors—from green to red to gold and brown. Smoke drifts from the chimneys of the surrounding farmhouses and there's a layer of frost on the grass—glittering bright in the faraway sun.

The bathroom door is off its hinges up top, so it drags on the concrete. There's a thick sludge across the floor. I almost slip, catching myself on the stained metal washbasin. I can feel the grit crunching under my boots. I go pee and smoke the butt of a cigarette I've been saving for a few days. I smoke and look at my reflection in the graffitied mirror.

My eyes are red and bloodshot around the blue. My skin is pale, framed by black, dirty-looking hair— since I didn't want to take a shower at the Super 8 motel before we left this morning. In the corner of the mirror someone has scratched FUCK YOU in all capital letters. I say it out loud.

"Fuck you."

I drop the cigarette in the sink and try to breathe, but this nausea won't leave me alone—this nausea that's been with me since she left. Since as long as I can remember.

There're oil fires burning through my insides.

I dig my nails into the palm of my hand, feeling the pain cutting in. At least it's a pain I can understand.

"Fuck. You," I say again. This time drawing out each word—my voice shaking.

From outside I hear the loud screeching of tires on wet pavement and then the sound of a heavy impact.

I struggle against the door and go running out into the shock of cold air.

On the one-lane highway in front of the diner, a pickup truck sits idling, gray smoke rising from the road behind it. The driver opens the door and steps out slowly. He is a stocky man, wearing a flannel shirt and a thicker flannel jacket. Steam comes in great gasps from his crooked nose and wide-open mouth.

Directly under the front tire of the pickup, a man

wearing tattered clothes, with dark skin and matted dark hair, lies motionless—crushed between the black rubber and the black asphalt. There is no blood. The man could very well be just sleeping there.

But he's not sleeping.

The driver walks over to the dead man. He stares down at the lifeless body. Then he looks up at me. His dark eyes stare straight into mine. His hands make little grabbing motions in the air. And he screams out. He screams louder than I've ever heard anyone scream in my whole life. He screams from somewhere deep in the very center of him. He screams from the center of him to the center of me.

"GET HELP!" he screams.

I turn back to the diner and burst into tears.

My dad has come running over. He presses me tightly against him, covering my eyes.

"Don't look," he whispers. "Don't look. Don't look."

But it's already too late.

The driver screams again.

I press my hands against my ears.

My dad rocks me back and forth in his arms.

"Shh," he tells me. "Shh."

I cry and cry.

I can't stop.

The tears are hot down my face.

I cry into my dad's sweatshirt.

I smell the smell of him.

The driver keeps on screaming behind us.

In my mind I see my mother lying there in front of me, her face blue and swollen—her eyes wide and red and bulging.

"It's all right," my dad says.

But I know that's a lie.

It's not all right.

It never will be again.

"I hate you," I tell him.

And when he asks me, "What?" I tell him, "Never mind."

It's late afternoon by the time we reach the house.

The sun is low on the distant horizon and it is still very cold.

My dad gets out of the car and unlocks the big padlock on the wrought iron gates with keys the owner must've given him.

We drive, not saying anything, up the uneven gravel driveway. There is a canopy of live oaks hanging with

Spanish moss. The wood is thick in all directions and green and shadowy. A shiver runs through me. The car skids and rattles. I see my dad's hands, veined and tight on the steering wheel. A mass of black crows or ravens are perched on the branches overhead. I dig my nails into the palms of my hands.

The house appears in a clearing beyond a line of bare white beech trees.

It is huge and dark and looming. The windows are black. And I am chilled.

"People actually pay to stay here?" I ask my dad, breaking the silence so my own voice sounds strange to me.

He smiles.

"It's not so bad."

The driveway curves around the house in a circle so we drive around to the back door and park. My dad shuts the car off and we both just sit there for a minute staring out.

"It's not for forever," he tells me.

We get out of the car.

"I'll show you around," my dad says.

"I gotta call Steph," I tell him. "They do have a phone here, don't they?"

"Of course."

I follow him up the crooked back stairs. He unlocks the door and steps inside. I grab hold of the screen and start in after him. But when my foot touches the threshold, something in my stomach turns cold and I stop. I look up at the uneven corners and mismatched, maniacal crossbeams and window frames and overhanging rooftops with dark wood shingles. There is no color anywhere. The whole house looks as if the life has been drained out of it.

And I don't want to go in.

"Dad," I say, faltering.

He turns and frowns.

"What?"

I search frantically in my mind for the right words.

"We shouldn't be here," I tell him.

He breathes out slowly.

"We've been over this. It's just for a little while. I know you didn't want to leave Johnstown."

"No, it's not that."

He steps back over to me and puts a hand on my shoulder.

"It's been a rough day," he says. "I understand. Come on in and call your friend. I'll show you around later."

I glance up at the enormous house looking down on me. It seems to be . . . watching. But that's just in my mind. And there's no reason not to come inside.

I close my eyes and walk through the open door.

The walls seem to rush in around me. As if I'd stayed still and it was the house that had moved to bring me inside.

But I am inside.

And I am okay.

Behind me the door slams shut and I jump a little.

He laughs.

"There's a phone in the kitchen. You'll feel better once you talk to Stephanie."

He pauses for a second before adding, "And, by the way, her mom said they might drive up for Thanksgiving. That's just a few weeks away."

I can see in his face how hard he's trying and I almost want to give in—to feel sorry for him. But I tell myself again that this is all his fault. He has—I have—no one else to blame. Cocksucker.

He reaches out to give me a hug, but I just walk on by.

The phone is in the kitchen, mounted on the bright-colored wall. It's actually a bright cheerful kitchen in general—which surprises me. There are hexagonal-shaped glasses in the cupboards. I drink water from the sink and fill a kettle with water and put it on to boil. There are boxes of tea next to the coffeemaker and plastic stirrers and sugar packets—I guess leftovers from the last guests who stayed here. I haven't checked the refrigerator yet, but I'm sure there's nothing much in it. My dad bangs in and out through the back door, unloading luggage and rearranging things.

I pick up the phone and dial.

It's Steph's mom, Lydia, who answers and I have to talk to her for a minute. I tell her about our trip—but leave out the dead guy underneath the pickup truck—before she finally puts Steph on.

Her voice is gentle sounding and familiar and I feel the pain of missing her in my chest—my heart beating faster.

"Is it terrible?" she asks.

"Yes," I say.

I tell her about the house and the drive and the man getting hit and then I start to cry again.

"Don't worry," she says. "It'll get better. It has to. And Mom says we're gonna come for Thanksgiving."

"Yeah, I know. My dad just told me. That'll be great."

"I'm excited to see the house," she says. "It sounds . . . creepy."

"It is."

I breathe in and out and tap my fingers on the counter and ask her, hesitating, "So . . . how's Todd?"

"You mean Turd?"

"Yeah. Him."

She hesitates, too, before speaking.

"He's still in the hospital."

"Jesus."

"I know."

Then she laughs and says, "The rumor around town is that you pushed him down those stairs."

I laugh, too.

"I wish I had. Asshole had it coming."

"You *sure* you didn't?"

I laugh more.

"You know Sunday mornings Dad does his weird church thing at our house. That's my alibi and I'm sticking to it."

She breathes out then, as if in relief—as if she actually considered that I could've pushed my ex-boyfriend down the stairs, breaking both his goddamn legs in the process.

"Well, good," she says.

"But if the town wants to believe I did it, that's fine with me."

"Speaking of people you'd like to push down the stairs," she says, "how's your dad doing?"

"The same," I say.

And then the teakettle starts screaming loudly on the gas stove.

I go over and turn the kettle off and make a cup of black tea with sugar.

"Have you seen the town yet?" Steph asks.

"We drove through it. I'm gonna walk in later. Looks pretty Podunk. And it's all shut down for the winter. Place is like a fuckin' ghost town."

"Alone with your dad in that big hotel all winter, huh?"

"Until you come visit."

"He starts writing, 'All work and no play makes Anselm a dull boy,' on a typewriter over and over? You get the hell out of there."

"It's gonna be *me* writing that," I say.

I sip the tea and burn my mouth.

"Ow, shit," I say.

From out in the hall I hear my dad call out, "I heard that."

I put my hand over the mouthpiece and yell back, "Sorry."

Steph laughs.

"All right, well . . . on that note. Call me after you check out the town, okay?"

"Yeah, I will."

And then I say, "You better come visit me soon."

I hang up and sit drinking tea for a minute before my dad comes in.

"How is she?" he asks.

I get up and stretch and crack my neck.

"She's fine."

"Good," he says. "You ready to see your room, then? I picked it out special."

"Yeah, all right, let me get my bag."

"I already brought it up there."

So I get up from the table and we walk together through the dark, complicated halls and passages. There seems to be no practical layout to the house at all. Bathrooms, parlors, living rooms, bedrooms—they are scattered haphazardly and lead strangely into one another. Some of the rooms have no windows at all. And some of the rooms have windows that only open out onto the main hallway. I guess that's what happens when they try turning some landmark house into a maximum-occupancy, superexpensive boutique hotel.

We climb the thick, mahogany staircase with the dark wooden banister. The walls seem to be leaning in on one another, like the whole place is some kind of sinking ship.

"I think a crazy person built this house," I say.

My dad smiles.

"That's part of its charm. The owners decided to keep it like this so the guests could experience what it was like to live in a real old Gothic-style mansion."

I look up at the triangular ceiling, which disappears into the shadows overhead.

"Were all Gothic mansions like this, then?" I ask.

"No, not necessarily. This house has a long and interesting history. I don't think anyone knows all of it."

We reach the third floor and turn down a long carpeted hallway with flowery wallpaper hung on either side. There are also some framed portraits—some of which, my dad says, actually belonged to the original family that built this place.

"Hey, that one looks like you," my dad says.

It's an oil painting of a young girl, maybe twelve or thirteen, with straight black hair, blue eyes, and pale, white skin. But she looks sickly somehow—like at the backs of her eyes—like there's something inside her trying to get out.

She's wearing a frilly white dress tight at the wrists. Her throat is tied with a bright red ribbon.

"I hope that's not what I look like," I say.

He laughs. "I'm just joking."

To get to the room my dad's decided is mine, we have to cut through a large, musty-smelling library, stacked high with leather-bound books.

"I'm gonna have to leave a trail of bread crumbs," I say, "if I ever want to find my way back."

He tells me I'll get used to it.

Though I pray to God I never do.

He opens the door and I almost have to squint, the room is so bright and pink. There's flowery wallpaper and a pink canopy bed hung with pink silk and pink curtains. The dresser is dark mahogany and so is the old-fashioned vanity.

"Well, what do you think?" my dad asks. "I figured it'd be perfect for my little girl."

My first instinct is to burst into tears, but I fight that back and instead just start to laugh. It's ridiculous, really—as if I were a little girl—as if I've ever worn anything pink or girly in my entire life.

My dad so clearly doesn't know me at all—or won't let himself know me. He only sees what he wants to see. It's the same goddamn thing he did with my mom.

There's no point fighting with him about it, so I go over to my suitcase on the bed and start to unpack, throwing shirts and jeans and sweaters into the dresser drawers.

"It's great," I tell him, with no conviction at all.

He opens the window wide and I feel the cold air coming in and smell the salt from the ocean.

"How close are we to the beach?" I ask.

He walks up behind me, taking my clothes out from the dresser and folding them neatly in a little pile.

"Just about half a mile. There's a path behind the house. We should take a walk down there later."

"Actually," I tell him, watching his knotted hands touching my clothes, "I wanted to walk into the town and check it out myself."

"Well, okay," he says, after thinking for a minute. "But this isn't a holiday, Jen. It's gonna take a lot of work maintaining this house through the winter. I've written out a list of chores I need you to do every day. And I'm going to be teaching your lessons every morning."

"I know," I tell him. "I'm going to work. And I'm going to study. But I have to have some fun. Anyway, I can pick up groceries for us. There's nothing in the house."

He nods, still folding my goddamn clothes.

"Yes, that would be good. I'll write you a list. This is going to be just what we need. I know it, Jen. This is really going to be perfect."

He glances down, then, and sees a tank top I'd forgotten I left in my suitcase. His hands reach out and he takes it up quickly.

"What is this?" he asks.

I try to grab the shirt back from him, but he pulls away.

"I don't know," I say. "Maybe it's Stephanie's."

His face turns very red and he stuffs the tank top in his jacket pocket.

"Don't lie to me," he yells. "Where did you get it?"

"I don't know. I'm telling you. I've never seen it before."

There are tears in my eyes now and I feel a pressure building inside.

"It's a *sin* to lie," he yells.

I grit my teeth and stare hatefully at him—wishing

more than anything that it could've been him—that *he* could've died instead of her.

"What is wrong with you?" he asks.

I stare and stare and wish him dead.

"This cannot go on like this," he shouts. "This cannot go on."

He grabs my bag from off the bed and dumps the contents out on the floor next to me. He sorts through them quickly, tossing them everywhere.

I stare hating him.

My teeth are clenched so tight my jaw aches.

I feel my heart pounding loud in my ears. There's a knife cutting in through the muscles in my stomach. I crack my neck and try to breathe but my chest is constricted and I press the palm of my hand into the center of my hot forehead.

"Dad," I say—trying to stay calm—speaking evenly. "Dad, that's enough."

He ignores me, of course. He goes on tearing through my things.

"Dad, stop it!" I yell.

I stomp my foot.

And then my dad cries out in pain. He clutches at his stomach and doubles over.

I turn to him, putting a hand on his back.

"Dad? What happened? Are you all right?"

I feel my hatred fading away.

He straightens, pushing me roughly.

"Hey!" I yell, falling back.

He gnashes his teeth.

"You're grounded," he says, spitting as he talks. "You're not going *anywhere!*"

He storms out of the room, slamming the door shut behind him.

"Asshole!" I say, but not so he can hear.

I gather up my clothes from off the floor, feeling like I might cry. The pain in my head has mostly gone. There's only the burning behind my eyes.

I go over to the window and look out at the surrounding forest. The sun is nearly set over the distant hills—the wind blowing in strong off the ocean.

For the first time I think that it really is very beautiful here—at least, outside of this goddamn house.

I watch as those same ravens land on the twisted branches of the trees below.

Squirrels chase one another across the grounds.

On the side of the house next to my window there is a white lattice built up almost to the roof, planted with crawling roses and rust-colored ivy. Who knows how long it's been there or how stable it is?

At this point, I really don't care.

In my suitcase there's a side zipper where I hid a photograph of my mom.

She has her hair down and is smiling—holding what must be a three- or four-year-old me in her arms. In this photo, at least, she looks happy. And I do, too. We look happy together. I like to think of my mom like this— smiling, holding me, brushing my hair. I remember the smell of her—like floral soaps and laundry detergent. When Dad would go into his rages—or the opposite of rages, when he would brood quietly—my stomach would be twisted up and the pain would cut in and my mom would come and sit with me in my bed. She'd get me to straighten my body out—to straighten my legs and lie flat so my stomach would unclench. She'd tell me to breathe—deeply—in and out. She'd smooth back my hair from my forehead. I'd feel the warmth of her delicate hand.

Then she'd read to me as I fell asleep. She'd read me that book *Eloise at the Plaza*. For some reason, as a kid, that book would always make me feel better. So my mom would read that to me. And she'd kiss me good night. And she'd try to protect me from my father. Though I guess she was the one who needed protection.

There are tears in my eyes now. I wipe them away and go hide the picture beneath my pillow. I go over to the window, staring out at the lattice structure. But then there is a voice coming from the room behind me—a woman's voice like my mother's.

"*Good-bye,*" it says.

I turn and look.

But I don't know why.

There can't be anything there.

I make my way slowly down the side of the house—the wooden structure shaking beneath my weight.

It's quiet outside except for the steady sound of the birds and crickets and the wind. I climb down into the tall grass and creep silently through the gray evening toward the stone garage.

A small cat appears underneath a tree that has initials carved in it, *AMJG.*

I crouch down and make a clicking noise and tap the ground with my hand, but the cat won't come to me.

Instead, a snap of a tree branch makes the cat dart off into the forest. I look up suddenly, and that's when I realize—someone else is watching.

CHAPTER 2

A figure, shadowed and dark but distinctly human, ducks behind the pitch pines grown close together at the edge of the clearing.

"Who's there?" I say, like an idiot.

No one answers.

My teeth start to chatter and I pull on my heavy jacket.

From behind the trees I see a flash of red and white, like someone wearing a kind of rugby jersey, maybe— someone tall, well over six feet.

"Hey, wait!" I yell.

There's the sound of wet leaves and pine needles underfoot and more branches snapping as the figure runs off through the forest.

"Wait."

I start to run after whoever it is but stop short at the line of trees.

The forest is very dark. The sky has turned gray and clouded overhead. The wind through the treetops scatters the leaves and strips bare the creaking branches. I hear the insane call of a woodpecker laughing, maniacal in the distance. There's a feeling like my stomach dropping out—like jumping off a high bridge into water, the way my friends and I used to when we'd take trips down to the Passaic. A strange smell comes from the entrance to the forest—a smell like something dead maybe, an animal rotting. And the cold from out of the dark becomes almost unbearable.

Even the cat, who's followed along beside me, seems leery of continuing on. It stands poised at the edge of the forest, swaying slightly and staring off as though hypnotized by the music of a snake charmer. Its eyes are yellow and watchful.

I force myself to laugh.

I pick the small cat up in my arms.

It begins to purr.

I carry it in the opposite direction, away from the smell and the forest and whoever it was behind the trees there.

"Do you have a home, or what?" I ask the cat.

I put it down next to a neatly stacked woodpile on the side of the house and then make my way back down the winding gravel path to the front gate we left open.

It takes me about ten minutes to walk into the town of Beach Haven—little more than tourist shops, a grocery store, a post office, an equestrian and hardware store, a library, a medical clinic, a dentist's office, a gas station, and a restaurant called the Double R Diner. The entire town spans the equivalent of two or three city blocks.

As of seven o'clock on a Wednesday night, the Double R Diner is the only establishment showing any signs of life. I walk there with my head down, doing my best to avoid my own darkened image in the reflection of a dull street lamp against the plate-glass windows. The engine of a large rusted pickup truck complains loudly as it drives slowly up the main road. A wiry, thin man with a reddish beard and hollowed-out features stares at me black-eyed and openmouthed.

I don't look away.

I imagine the red-bearded man and the driver both falling dead and the truck running off the road—careening through the darkened window of the Beach Haven Pharmacy and Five & Dime.

The sky is black and starless, with the pale fingernail of a moon obscured by racing clouds.

The truck lumbers on up the road.

The neon sign for the Double R Diner blinks red and orange—on and off, on and off. I have a little money saved up from my job last summer working at the bookstore in Johnstown, so I figure I'll go in and get a coffee and maybe something to eat.

The diner is relatively spacious with red vinyl booths set up along the walls, a few tables, a counter with built-in stools and a bright flashing jukebox in the corner playing twangy-sounding cowboy music. An elderly couple, both with skin like yellowed wax paper and heavy-lidded bloodshot eyes, turn to look up at me. So do the truck drivers at the counter and the old woman sitting by herself wearing a mass of thick sweaters and one of those long quilted barn coats. The gray-haired waitress behind the counter puts down her pot of coffee to look at me, too. No one smiles. I set my jaw tight. I wish I were back home. I imagine the diner on fire, all of them running out screaming as flames spread from floor to ceiling.

The cowboy song on the jukebox fades out. There is an interminable silence before the next song is queued up. I think about walking out. But I don't. I go sit at the counter. The waitress comes over and offers me coffee from a deeply stained, chipped coffeepot.

"Thank you," I tell her.

"You wanna see a menu?" she asks, her voice hoarse-sounding. "We have a meat loaf special."

I shake my head.

"No, thank you."

She pours the coffee. I add milk from the pitcher and two packs of sugar. It's good coffee. Hot.

The door behind me dings open.

A girl, probably around my age, but with blond hair and a sickeningly cheery smile, comes bouncing over next to me.

She gives the waitress a hug, leaning her long, slender body over the counter.

"What are you doing here?" the old woman asks her. "Did you eat yet?"

The girl smiles even bigger.

"I wanted to come see you. And Dad said you baked a huckleberry pie. There any left?"

The waitress laughs.

"Thought that might be it."

"Well, I wanted to see you, *too*," the girl says.

"I know," the old woman tells her. "Come sit down. I put a piece aside for you. You want it hot? With vanilla ice cream?"

"Yes, please."

The girl sits down at the counter.

Then she turns to me.

"Oh, hello," she says. "What's your name?"

"Uh, I'm Jen," I say.

"I'm Christy. Are you on vacation here?"

I take a sip of ice water, feeling a little flushed for some reason.

"Uh, no," I say. "I . . . I just moved here. My dad's gonna be the caretaker of that old Harmony House place."

Christy gets even brighter and cheerier and her general positive whatever is kind of freaking me out, if you want to know the truth.

"Harmony House? Cool."

She turns to the waitress again.

"Hey, Aunt Rose, did you hear that? This is the girl living with her dad up in Harmony House."

"I heard," says the waitress—her aunt—Rose—I guess.

She sets the pie and ice cream down in front of Christy and, I have to admit, the smell is pretty damn incredible.

She turns to me, studying my face like she's trying to figure out . . . I don't even know what.

"How's it going up there so far?" she asks.

I try to smile.

"Fine," I say. "We only just got in today."

"And you're staying here all through the winter?" she asks.

I nod, half watching Christy eating that pie with a look that must give away how hungry I am, because Rose laughs to herself and then tells me, "Hold on," and starts making up another plate for me.

"Thank you," I tell her. "I haven't eaten all day."

"Aunt Rose's pies," says Christy, smiling. "The cornerstone of every nutritious meal."

I take a bite and smile, too. "It's good," I tell her.

She pats me awkwardly on the head.

"Sweet of you to say."

I drink the hot good coffee and eat the hot good pie.

Christy and her aunt both laugh at how hungry I am.

"So are you gonna be startin' high school here?" Christy asks me. "At Beach Haven?"

I shake my head.

"Uh, no," I say, haltingly. "I'm gonna be . . . uh . . . taking a break, I guess. I'm supposed to be a junior. But . . . uh . . . my mom died a couple months ago, so . . ."

I trail off—not sure why the hell I just let that out of my mouth. I take another bite of pie to try to shut myself up.

"Oh God," Christy says, startled. "That's terrible! I'm so sorry."

She puts a small, fragile-looking hand on my shoulder.

"Yeah, no," I say, stumbling over my words. "It's been hard, but . . ."

"Well, I tell you what," she says. "I'm working at my family's store down the block all winter—selling beads."

I make a face. "Bees?"

She laughs.

"B-e-a-d-s. Ye Olde Bead Shoppe. Most businesses close this time of year. But we're open right up 'til Christmas and then all through January. 'Cause, you know, people might have . . . *bead emergencies* . . . I guess."

I can't help but laugh a little at that, too.

"I'm there most days after school gets out," she says. "You come by any time you need anything, okay?"

"Thank you," I say. "That's super sweet. Are you a senior?"

"Yeah," she tells me. "Doing all the college application stuff right now."

I groan.

"So not looking forward to that."

"Well, at least you've got a good thing to write an essay about."

She covers her mouth, flushing a bright red.

"Sorry, that wasn't funny."

"No, you're right," I say. "Some girl at my old school got attacked by a bear while she was on one of those Outward Bound trips and she got into every school she applied to. Maybe you should just pretend you're a bulimic cutter with ADHD, OCD, and bipolar disorder."

Christy keeps on blushing.

"Believe me, I've thought about it. But I'm sorry just the same. That was a stupid joke."

I tell her, again, that it's really okay.

We continue on talking for a while more—eating pie, drinking coffee, and listening to the twangy cowboy music coming from the jukebox.

"Maybe you'd like to come over sometime?" Christy says.

"Yeah, I'd like that," I tell her, trying to be polite and all. "If my dad lets me."

Aunt Rose comes over then and refills our coffees and presses her wide, wrinkled, hand with the knotted blue veins down on the Formica countertop.

"You be sure to make him," she says, surprising me that she'd been listening to our conversation. "You don't want to let yourself get too isolated living up in that house just the two of you."

"I couldn't agree more," I say.

"Really should've burned that place down years ago," she says—more to herself than to me.

"Oh, you hush now, Aunt Rose. There's nothing wrong with that house."

She turns to me then and says, "Aunt Rose used to work there when she was a girl. Don't pay any attention to her."

I force a smile, not sure what the hell they're talking about.

"Well, in any case," says Rose, handing me a paper menu. "Here's our phone number if you need anything. And, here, I'll write my niece's number and my home number on the back, too."

And then she adds, "Please don't hesitate to call either one of us."

I thank them both, thinking that if everyone in this little town is as nice as these two, then maybe Beach Haven won't be so bad after all. I stand and try to pay, but Rose won't let me. I fold the menu up and put it in the side pocket of my black parka.

Outside it is cold, so I pull my hood up over my head and put on a pair of woolen fingerless gloves. The moon has risen higher and there is the steady sound of dry leaves rattling in the dark. I can hear a train whistle way off in the distance.

There's a path behind the diner that winds through an overgrown field of weeds and dead blackberry bushes. A smell like damp and rot rises up from the ground.

At the edge of the town there is a group of boys standing huddled against the back of the feed store smoking cigarettes—the burning orange embers glowing like coals in the hearth of a smoldering fire.

"Hey," I say, walking closer. "Hey, you guys got an extra cigarette?"

It's three of them in all—tall, muscular-looking boys wearing baseball hats and Carhartt jackets. They are handsome, I guess, in a frat-boy kind of way—but I'm definitely getting kind of a date-rapey vibe from the three of them.

"Where'd you come from?" the biggest of the three asks me.

"Just from the diner there," I say.

He snorts a laugh.

"No. I mean, where you from? I know you ain't from around here . . . gorgeous."

I roll my eyes.

"Okay, never mind," I say.

I start off walking in the direction of the house. From behind me I hear the boys' muffled voices discussing something. I try to walk a little faster, back out onto the main street, where, at least, it's not totally dark—even if it is completely fucking empty. There isn't a single other person or car in the street.

Only I can hear footsteps coming up behind me.

It's that first boy I talked to. He's by himself, which is a small relief, but not a big one.

"Wait up," he says, a little out of breath. "I didn't mean to scare you off. I'm Alex."

He gets in front of me and extends his hand for me to take it. His broad face is covered in a constellation of freckles and somehow that works to make him seem a little less threatening.

When I don't take his hand right away he says, "Aw, come on. I was just messing around. And, anyway, what's the big deal? You *are* gorgeous."

"I gotta go," I tell him.

He keeps on traipsing along beside me.

"How 'bout this," he says. "If I can figure out who you are in . . . uh . . . three guesses, then you have to agree to let me walk you home. What do you think about that?"

I shake my head.

"I think you probably already know who I am, considering there are about twelve people in this whole goddamn town."

He laughs.

"Yeah, okay. You got me. You're the girl whose dad is taking care of Harmony House through the winter, right? You just got here today?"

I slow my pace down.

"Yup. That's right."

"Well, what's your name?" he asks. "Will you give me that, at least?"

"You can't guess that?"

He takes off his Yankees baseball hat and runs his long, thick fingers through his blondish-brown hair. He's wearing too much of some cheap cologne and it kind of gives me a headache.

"All right," he says. "Just stop for a second. I'll try."

I stop walking and turn toward him.

"Okay," he continues, squinting his eyes and reaching his hands up to me like a carnival fortune-teller getting messages straight from the goddamn cosmos.

He starts mumbling some different vowels and consonants, stretching out the sound and watching me closely as though I might tip him off when he's getting close. "Mmmm, Nnnn, Geeeeeee, Aaaaa, Beeeeee, Kaaaaay, Llll, Eeeee, Jaaaaaay . . . Jen?"

"What?" I say, genuinely surprised.

"Jen? Is it Jen?"

Now it's my turn to squint at him.

"Someone must've told you," I say.

"No, I guessed."

"Well, I am dubious," I tell him. "But I guess a deal's a deal."

"Here," he says, handing me the cigarette I'd forgotten I'd asked for.

"Oh, thanks."

I take it and do the whole lighting-a-cigarette thing. I breathe in and out.

"Listen," I say. "You can walk me to the gate, but you really can't come any farther. My dad . . . he's kind of old-fashioned. If he sees me walking with a boy, he really might kill you and me both. That's no joke."

Alex seems to puff up slightly.

"I ain't scared of nobody."

"Yeah, well, you might wanna rethink that."

I start walking again and he follows right up next to me.

"Are you a senior, too?" I ask. "I just met that girl Christy whose aunt works at the diner. I guess you must know her."

"Yeah," he says. "I've lived here my whole life. Me 'n Christy been in school together since kindergarten. Same with Matt and Charlie, my two friends back there. What about you? What grade are you in?"

I tell him.

"So you're seventeen?" he asks—saying it like he's disappointed I'm not, you know, *legal*, yet. It creeps me out. Especially because we're already through town and on the winding road back to Harmony House—walking under the canopy of low-hanging trees and moss.

"What do you think about living in a haunted house?" he asks—the question startling me a little.

"A haunted house?" I say. "What do you mean?"

He laughs. "You didn't know it was haunted?"

I try to laugh, too, but it doesn't come out right.

"Uh, no," I say, sounding as casual as I can. "I didn't."

"Oh yeah," he says. "No one in town will go up there."

"What was Harmony House?" I ask. "Do you know? Before it was a hotel?"

I drag on my cigarette and exhale and listen to the night noises from the forest around us.

"There are a lot of different stories. Some say the family that built it, their daughter, who was like our age, actually . . . she committed suicide in the house."

"Jesus Christ."

"Yeah. Then I heard it was like a home for unwed mothers—run by the Catholic church. Supposedly there's a graveyard out back with all the dead babies and mothers who died in childbirth."

"Jesus."

"I've never seen it, though."

"You looked?"

He smiles.

"Sure, yeah. When I was a kid, me 'n my friends would come 'round here on dares and stuff. It wasn't a hotel then—just a big . . . you know . . . abandoned house."

He stares off for a moment before adding quickly, "But we never found anything. No graves. No ghosts."

"Great," I say. "You really know how to welcome a girl to the neighborhood."

He laughs.

We've reached the wrought iron gate now and I turn to say good-bye to him.

"Aw, come on," he says. "I'll walk you a little farther. Your dad won't find out."

"No, I can't. Seriously."

I step in front of him, kind of, to block his path, but he keeps on walking around me, through the gate, looking around and saying, "Wow, I haven't been up here in a long time."

"Look," I tell him. "I really have to go."

He smiles. The trees along the driveway cast his face in shadows.

"Which room are you staying in?" he asks. "I could come climb up and see you later?"

"Uh, yeah, not gonna happen," I say.

He laughs.

"I'm serious."

"I'm serious, too."

"Don't you like me?"

"I just met you."

"We could have some fun," he says.

He leans in close to me in the dim light, like he's trying to kiss me and for the first time I realize that he must actually be kind of drunk, or something, because his breath smells like some kind of hard alcohol. I take a step back.

"Come on, man, be cool," I say.

His look isn't really the nicest look I've ever seen.

In fact, it's a look that makes me chilled all over.

"Anyway, I gotta go," I say again.

I turn and start to run off down the trail.

But then he catches me by the wrist and pulls me back toward him. A sick feeling forms at the base of my stomach. My heart races. I contemplate kicking him in the balls but hesitate for some reason.

"You don't go until I tell you to go," he says.

His eyes are wide and crazy-looking in the darkness. I pivot and swing my boot up with all the force I can gather under it, connecting with the side of his leg so he doubles over and yells, "You bitch!" but then is up fast and running after me as I sprint down the driveway.

We round the bend, him close up behind me, when I give a little shriek and stop because a new boy has just stepped out onto the road. Me and Alex must see him at the same time, because we both stop running and I can feel his hot breath on me and my heart really does feel like it's about to crawl up out of my throat and go running off screaming into the woods.

The new boy steps past me, wordlessly, and punches Alex straight in the face—sending blood shooting out of both nostrils and making him sit down hard on the cracked concrete.

"Leave, now," I hear the new boy say and I turn to see Alex push himself up and go running off down the driveway.

The new boy comes over to me, a little out of breath.

"Hey," he says. "You all right?"

I shake my head.

"No," I say. "No, I'm not."

I blink my eyes and try to focus on him. He's heavily

built with big, broad features and dark skin.

"But thank you."

He nods slowly and then I notice the red kind-of rugby shirt with a white stripe he's wearing.

"Hey, were you in the woods back here earlier?" I ask.

He laughs.

"Yeah, there's a path that goes through there from the beach into town. I'm sorry. I didn't mean to sneak up on you."

"It's all right," I say. "I just moved in today . . . so, uh . . . I don't know the area."

"Yeah, I know," he says.

He smiles more and I can see a dimple in his cheek that's pretty goddamn cute.

"Everyone's been talking about you coming into town. There's not much else going on 'round here."

"So I gathered."

"I'm Colin, by the way," he says.

I tell him my name and we shake hands and I feel the heat from his body.

"I'm sorry about Alex," he says. "His dad owns like ninety percent of the real estate in Beach Haven . . . and Staffordshire Township. He's used to getting what he wants. The whole Winter family is like that."

"Winter?"

"Yeah, Alex Winter. He's got three brothers and they're all as bad as he is. Worse, maybe."

"Isn't that the name of the actor in *Bill & Ted's Excellent Adventure*? I mean, the one who's not Keanu Reeves?"

Colin laughs again.

"I never saw it."

"Well, thank you, again," I say. "Are you gonna have trouble with him later?"

He shrugs.

"Twenty bucks says he won't even remember this. We were on the football team together a couple of years ago. I can handle him fine."

"There was something not right about him," I say. "I felt that right off."

"Everyone's goin' a little crazy with the winter coming in. Town like this, there's nothin' to do 'til spring. You'll see. It'll probably get worse before it gets better."

"Great," I say.

We both stay silent for a minute.

"How long have you lived here?" I ask him, starting back toward the house, letting him walk along with me.

"Couple years," he says. "I was in Vermont before

this. My uncle's a contractor. Did some work on the Harmony House remodel, actually."

"Oh," I say. "So you know it, then?"

"Yeah, a little. My uncle only lasted a couple days on the job. You know there are no right angles in the entire building? Every corner is off center. And a room that seems like it should be directly on top of another room is to the left or right. It's like a carnival fun house. The original owner built it that way intentionally, so the hotel developers wanted to preserve that same . . . uh . . . lack of symmetry." He pauses. "Which, when you're in construction, is a real pain in the ass."

I laugh. "Is that why your uncle quit?"

"No, not just that. You meet him? The developer guy?"

"No."

"People here wanted to run him out of town. They were pretty unhappy with the house being turned into a tourist attraction. There're a lotta stories about what went on up there. They think the place should have been . . . left alone."

I glance down the drive toward the house. "Thanks for your help," I say. "But I better go on alone from here. I was trying to explain this to our mutual pal Alex, there, but my dad is a bit of a Puritan. Meaning if he sees me walking with a boy, he's gonna come kill me and then kill said boy, and then we're both gonna be dead."

He laughs. "You sure you're all right?"

I nod.

"Well, it's a small town," he says. "So I know I'll see you again."

"I hope so. I really can't thank you enough."

I stand on my tiptoes and kiss his rough-feeling cheek—quickly.

I run off then without saying anything else.

I run down the dark, winding driveway, the trees like a canopy overhead. There is a crashing through the underbrush. Rats and night birds, screeching owls, the high-pitched cries of bats in the night.

A car engine sounds behind me and there are headlights rounding the bend. It must be my dad returning from the store. I cut off the road into the tangle of branches and ivy. I crouch in the bramble, waiting, holding my injured wrist tightly.

My dad's car drives slowly by.

I bide my time.

My eyes struggle to adjust to the darkness again after the lights pass.

I creep back toward the house.

I climb up the trellis again and in through my open window.

The room is just as pink and terrible as when I left it.

I take off my contraband clothes and hide them under the bed.

Then I put on a pair of flannel pajamas and get out my cosmetics bag with my toothbrush and makeup.

I open the heavy door to my room and step out into the strange, curving hallway lined with grotesque, mismatching wallpaper. The closest bathroom is down the hall and so I walk clumsily.

From behind me I hear the faintest of whispering.

It's like a breath, a sigh from somewhere just out of sight.

My heart beats painfully fast, though I can't say why.

"Hello?" I say, my voice cracking.

The whispering comes again—words I can't quite make out.

"Who's there?" I ask.

The sound again—too faint and mumbled.

My hands shake.

And, finally, I recognize the voice.

My vision blurs with tears.

The voice . . .

It is my mother's.

I feel the plush blue carpet from our house in Johnstown under my feet as I walk down the staircase. The front door is open, letting in the damp summer heat. Two uniformed police officers stand, arms crossed, heads bowed, talking to my father. The lights from the cruiser outside blink red then blue then red again. The officer speaks softly, but not so softly that I can't hear.

"I'm sorry. She didn't make it."

And now, in Harmony House, I hear my mother again.

"Anselm," she whispers.

But it can't be true.

It can't.

I follow the sound down the hallway. It seems to be coming from the room just in front of me.

I try the doorknob, but for some reason it's locked.

I try it again.

And then something grabs me from behind.

CHAPTER 3

"What are you doing?"

It's my father, his eyes narrowed at me.

"Dad, what the h . . . heck? You scared me."

"Where are you going?" he asks, his jaw set.

"Nowhere," I say. "I just—I thought I heard something in here."

"Heard what?"

My mind goes blank, searching for an answer. The whispering has stopped now. And it obviously wasn't my mother. It can't have been. I don't know what the hell is wrong with me.

"Why's this door locked?" I ask, trying to change the subject.

He tries the knob himself, as if he doesn't believe me.

"Huh? Well, maybe they put some of the valuables in here. Let's see . . ."

He rummages around in his pocket and pulls out an antique-looking skeleton key.

"This should do it," he says.

He fits the key in the lock and turns the bolt.

The door is heavy, but I force it open. The smell from inside comes wafting out and my dad and I both recoil.

"Did something die in here?" I say stupidly.

"Yeah, maybe."

I step through the door. A shiver runs through me. The temperature has dropped like twenty degrees just in this room—even though the windows are closed.

The dust and cobwebs are thick on the white sheets draped over the furniture. Otherwise, the room is like some kind of antiques store. Old, valuable-looking lamps and paintings stand on every surface. There are stacks of books and fine china and silver. A large Oriental rug is rolled up in the corner.

A small leather-bound book sits by itself on an antique dressing table. I stare, somehow unable to take my eyes from it.

"See? The valuables," my dad says. "At least we don't have to clean in here."

He laughs, the noise sounding strangely hollow—forced.

My dad goes to the windows and checks the locks. I go to the book and pick it up quickly. It drops neatly into the pocket of my robe.

I'm not sure why I do it, exactly, except I'm curious. There seems to be something about it—I don't know what.

"Well, come on," he says. "I made some dinner—it's our first night, so it's just grilled cheese sandwiches. Tomorrow I'll make something better."

"Sure," I say. "Thanks, that'd be great."

"And we'll lock this back up."

"Okay."

"Okay."

I look at my dad in this cold, shivering room. He is trying. I can see that. He may be a backward, judgmental religious asshole—but he is my dad.

I laugh then.

"What's funny?" he asks, smiling.

"Nothing," I say. "Thanks for making dinner."

He shuts the door behind us and we step back out into the hallway—away from that rotting smell and the icy cold.

Downstairs we sit in the brightly painted kitchen eating grilled cheese sandwiches and half-burnt zucchini. The simple food is good on my stomach after the pie and ice cream earlier. I drink a ginger ale and my dad drinks a bottle of Budweiser.

"I got donuts for the morning, too," he says.

I thank him, though the thought of anything sweet right now makes my stomach turn.

"I really want this to be a fresh start for you," he says. "I want it to be a fresh start for both of us."

"Yeah," I say lamely.

"I'm sorry things have been so hard."

I sip the ginger ale—then, awkwardly, put my hand on his.

"They've been hard for you, too, Dad. I know that. We both miss her."

"But it's not just that," he says, clasping both his hands around mine. "I need you to understand."

He looks into my eyes and I look away.

"Your mother and I," he says. "We weren't on the righteous path. She was a sinner. She squandered the many gifts God gave her. She brought us down. She would have pulled us both into the pit of hell. Now we have this chance and . . . I need to take advantage of it. I need you to take advantage of it, too. We're so fortunate to have it—"

I pull my hand free of his.

My jaw sets tight and I speak through gritted teeth.

"Fortunate. We're *fortunate*."

"Yes, don't you see? God's given us this opportunity to repent."

I stare hard at him.

We are fortunate, he says, that my mother is dead.

We are fortunate, he says, and he means it.

I want to scream. I want to scream at him and hit him. I want to wake him the fuck up.

The sickness is back in my stomach. The heat rises inside of me.

The yellow kitchen walls and framed black-and-white photographs of lighthouses spin around me.

"We have a responsibility," he says. "To practice His principles day in and day out. Your mother wouldn't listen to me. She wouldn't listen to anybody. But I won't let that happen to you. Your soul's salvation is my responsibility."

I stand, clenching my fists, and breathe in. The heat flushes my cheeks and for just a moment my whole body seems as though it's on fire.

A loud crash sounds just behind me.

My father gasps and shields his face.

The heat drains as quickly as it came. I turn, startled.

"What was that?"

"Careful," my dad says. "You're not wearing any shoes."

A glass bowl has broken into tiny pieces all across the linoleum. It is so thoroughly shattered, it looks like spilled granules of sugar.

"Careful," my dad says again.

The wave of anger is gone, replaced by a deep weariness. I am so tired I just want to curl up in a corner somewhere and disappear.

"I'm not feeling well," I tell him. "I'm going to bed."

He looks distractedly at me and then back at the puzzle of broken glass.

"What? Yeah, okay."

I walk out into the hallway. The smell of mold is dank and cloying beneath the shadowed stairwell. A cold shiver runs through me and I wrap my arms tightly around myself.

Then a sharp pain cuts into the center of my forehead.

I squeeze my eyes shut against it.

When I open my eyes again, a flash of movement makes me turn.

In the very corner of my vision there is a figure in white. A girl in a flowing dress.

She glides across the floor as though floating back and forth, back and forth, to a gentle rhythm.

Her long black hair hangs down, contrasted starkly with the white of her dress and her pale skin.

I move my lips to call for help.

But the words won't come.

And then I see a rope, caked with dirt and blood, around her throat. It extends up, to a railing above us.

Her eyes are bloodshot and bulging—her tongue protruding blue. Her neck elongated.

I blink and stumble backward. When I turn to look again, the girl's body is gone. There is nothing in front of me but empty space.

I shiver all over, wondering—was I asleep?

Was I dreaming?

I start up the many flights of stairs, back to the

upstairs bathroom—trying to forget whatever the hell *that* just was.

Inside the bathroom there is a separate walk-in shower and a deep claw-foot tub. I scrub my face at the sink and pick at a couple zits on my forehead and brush my teeth.

Behind me, I can see in the mirror's reflection, a framed woodblock print of a sperm whale—like from the cover of *Moby Dick*. There's also a horizontal, rectangular triptych of different sailboats and another frame with mounted pieces of rope tied in various sailing knots—each knot with its own handwritten label beneath it. I study them absently—the bolan, the double half hitch, the hangman's knot.

Tomorrow, I tell myself, I will go down to the beach.

I spit the foaming toothpaste in the sink and drink some water straight from the faucet—cool and clean-tasting.

I put on some lip gloss.

And then I remember the little hardbound book in my pocket. I take it out and squint to read the faded markings engraved in the cover. *Devotions of Saint Francis of Assisi.*

Inside, the first pages contain the prayer my father has drilled into my head a million times:

Lord, make me an instrument of Your
    peace
Where there is hatred, let me sow love
Where there is injury, pardon
Where there is discord, harmony
Where there is error, truth
Where there is doubt, faith
Where there is despair, hope
Where there is darkness, light
And where there is sadness, joy.
O Divine Master, grant that I may not
    so much seek
To be consoled as to console
To be understood as to understand
To be loved as to love.
For it is in giving that we receive
It is in pardoning that we are pardoned
And it is in dying that we are born to
    eternal life.

Many other, less familiar prayers follow, along with illustrations of Saint Francis himself surrounded by woodland creatures—the animals gathered around him, birds perched on his fingers and shoulders like he's some kind of goddamn Disney princess.

I flip quickly through and land on the inside back cover.

A name has been penciled in on the thick, rough-textured endpaper. I read the inscription—

Margaret.

I snap the book shut and throw it on the floor.

Margaret. My mother's name.

My mother's name is written in the cover of the book. It is written in the same kind of perfect, feminine handwriting she always had.

I sink down onto the bathroom rug.

The house sounds fade out.

Everything blurs around me.

Images are projected on the backs of my eyelids.

Gray morning light seeping in around the edges of plush, red velvet curtains. A small boy, dark-haired, with shining blue eyes and pale white skin, sits on the frayed Oriental rug looking up at a young woman in a black tunic with her long blond hair hanging down her back. She holds a nun's habit in her hands and stares down, lovingly, at the boy.

The images flash and stutter like film running through an old-fashioned movie projector—jumping from frame to frame, skipping and tearing in places.

But I recognize the room.

It's where I found the book—here, in Harmony House. Only it is different. Crosses are nailed to the bare white walls. The boy plays absently with a string of rosary beads. A fire burns, flickering in the hearth.

The woman—a nun, I realize—retrieves a brush from the antique bureau and begins to sweep it through her long, shining hair. She sings softly to herself—and to the boy.

"You're beautiful," the boy tells her.

She turns and smiles.

"What a nice thing to say."

The boy reaches out his hand to her.

"Are you my mother?" he asks.

The woman presses her lips together.

"You don't remember?"

The boy shakes his head.

She takes his hand in hers.

"Your mother is with the angels in Heaven," she says. "But I love you just as much as if you were my own child. And I will always love you. And I will always care for you. And I will never let you go."

"I love you, too," says the boy.

The woman ties her hair back now and secures the habit over her head.

"The babies will need to be fed and changed," she says. "Will you come with me to heat the bottles?"

The boy nods.

"Is that girl still here?" he asks.

The woman stops adjusting the buttons on her habit and stares at him.

"Which girl?"

"The one who was screaming last night?"

The woman gets down low next to the boy and whispers, "Hush, now. Hush. Don't let the monsignor or the other sisters hear you talk about that."

"But . . . she was screaming and . . ."

The woman shakes her head.

"She's gone up to Heaven, baby."

"With my mommy?"

"Yes."

The boy gets to his feet and then bends to tie his shoe. The woman takes the laces from him and ties them herself.

From down the hall, heavy footsteps sound, creaking the floorboards, growing rapidly closer.

"Quick," says the woman. "Under the bed. Go. Hide!"

The boy's eyes go wide with something like terror. He stumbles quickly beneath the wooden bed frame and threadbare mattress, peering out from underneath. He watches as the woman, now fully dressed in her habit, goes to tend the fire. The door swings open. Another nun, older, with rimless glasses and deep furrows around her mouth, steps into the room.

"What are you still doing here?" the older nun demands. "The babies need tending."

"Yes, Sister," the woman says. "I was worried about sparks from the fire. But I've fixed it now. I'll start making up the bottles."

"See that you do," the older nun says.

She slams the door.

The woman turns toward the bed.

"Okay," she says. "You can come out now."

But the boy remains hidden, soaked with sweat and trembling cold.

CHAPTER 4

I wake up on the cold tile floor with a feeling like a drill boring into the center of my forehead. My teeth grit together and I press the palm of my hand against my temple. I pull myself up to standing and drink water from the faucet. A wave of nausea sweeps through me. I clutch at my stomach and gag.

The vision—if that's what it was—replays itself over and over in my mind. The pretty nun, the little boy, the way he hid trembling under the bed. It was like it was all happening there in front of me. Like it had all happened in this house a long time ago.

But that doesn't make any sense.

It must've just been a nightmare.

Or maybe some kind of fever dream. Because I'm sick as hell.

I cough and retch and gag over the sink.

I splash water on my face and try to breathe.

When I close my eyes I can still see that older nun with her face all lined and full of hatred. In the image I have of her now her eyes are black, scribbled out, and dead-looking.

I face myself in the mirror. What the hell am I thinking?

You're crazy, I tell myself.

"You're crazy," I say out loud.

Then I open my mouth and look down my throat and gnash my teeth. "Get it together," I say.

I open the bathroom door and see that the house is dark. It feels very late—or maybe very early. I make my way back to the pink Pepto-Bismol room, crawling under the thick down comforter. I lie there until the nausea passes. I drift off to sleep. And in sleep, I dream.

I dream of my mom.

When she picked me up from school in our old

green Volvo station wagon—surprising me, since I usually had to stay in the after-school program. She was so pretty then. Her eyes were blue and she smiled big—her two front teeth pushed in a little so it made her canines stand out sharp and feline-looking. She had a small, angular nose and high cheekbones and a narrow jaw. Her neck was long and elegant and she wore a silver cross necklace. She took my backpack from me, and I had to reach up to take her hand.

Driving through the bright spring afternoon, she played David Bowie's *Aladdin Sane* on the six-CD changer and we both sang along. The surrounding country was coming back to life green and vibrant after the long winter. In the parks families were out walking their dogs and kids were playing pickup baseball games and people were out boating on the lake.

My mom had the windows rolled down and we sang together as we passed through downtown and drove out the old highway to the thrift store owned by my mom's friend Mrs. Douglas—who would call my mom and tell her when she got in special fabrics, clothes, or records. My mom was a seamstress and would sew dresses for me.

She never got to use her talents as much as she liked,

working the way she did at the makeup counter at Pee-bles. But she was very talented. That day she bought a length of bright, floral-patterned fabric she would make into a blouse and a pair of matching shorts for me. And she let me buy a Jackson 5 record they had on sale for a dollar.

Then, on the way home, we stopped to get ice cream and she told me not to tell my dad, because it would ruin my dinner. Then she stopped at the packaged goods store and bought something in a brown paper bag for herself. Dad didn't know about that either.

We had a lot of secrets like that. We had to hide so many things from him.

Though, eventually, she started hiding things from me, too.

And soon she disappeared from both of us com-pletely.

But in my dream, I remember her as she was before.

Sitting on the bench outside the ice-cream parlor, my legs dangling, swinging back and forth.

She laughed and told me stories about when she'd been my age and how she used to chase the boys in school and try to kiss them. She told me that when she caught one boy and kissed him on the cheek, he burst into tears and went and told the teacher and she got in trouble.

"I want you to promise me something," she said, the flash of her smile gone—her eyes unblinking, staring straight into me. "Promise me you'll make better decisions than I did."

Wanting to say the right thing, I nodded and told her yes. I promised that of course—*of course* I would.

"You know I love you more than anything in the world," she continued. "But I want you to have choices, okay? Don't ever let anyone make you feel like you don't have choices. You always do."

And then she stopped looking at me and turned to stare at something far-off. She added, dully, with a half smile, "Until you don't."

And I didn't know what she meant, but I shivered— maybe just from the ice-cream cold in my chest. And I reached out my hand and touched hers. And she laughed and hugged me tight against her and I could smell that smell of her again and feel the warmth in her embrace.

I was happy.

Maybe we both were.

Until we weren't.

◻ ◻ ◻

In the morning I feel sick as hell again and I want to stay in bed, but my dad is pounding on the door, telling me to get up.

I try to do what he says, but the pain in my head is really unbearable.

I turn and lie back down again.

The door opens and my dad comes in—like he does every goddamn morning—so we can pray together.

"Dad," I say. "Please, I'm not feeling good."

He tells me prayer will heal whatever is wrong with me.

I want to tell him to fuck off, but, of course, I don't, because that would just make everything worse. So I follow him downstairs to his dank room. The musty smell of it is overwhelming—like some kind of mold rotting beneath the floorboards.

"Can I at least go to the bathroom first?" I ask him.

He says for me to wait.

Against one wall of his bedroom he's erected a kind of altar with a giant cross showing, in exact detail, the nails driven in and the crown of thorns and the blood dripping down.

My dad gets on his knees and gestures for me to do the same.

It's a ritual I'm used to at this point.

He prays out loud, asking for God's forgiveness and saying we're not worthy and blah, blah, blah. Pretty boring stuff. But my dad is all emotional about it and I think he might even cry—I can hear a tremor in his voice.

"And please, Lord," he says. "Save my daughter. Show her the path to salvation that she may not spend eternity burning in the fires of hell."

I keep my head down.

My dad drones on and on.

Then another voice whispers in my ear.

"*Sinner*," it hisses.

I close my eyes and shake my head to clear it.

Finally, though, my dad finishes talking. He says, "Amen," and I say it, too.

I go back upstairs to the bathroom and try to wash my face, but the pain in my head is so bad now I can barely open my eyes. It's not the easiest thing in the goddamn world, but I manage to get back to my room and I sort of stumble over to the closet. There's a bag of pills that Steph and I stole from her dad's medicine cabinet in the lining of my navy blue peacoat.

Staring at the pills now, they're all kinds of pastel multicolors—Vicodin, Percocet, Xanax, some opiate—I can't remember what it's called.

I reach into the plastic bag and take one of the thick, round Percocet and dry-swallow it before going back to the bathroom to drink water from the faucet.

Looking up into the mirror, I see my reflection in the mirror is kind of a train wreck. I'm strangely thin— my face pale and sunken around the eyes and jawline. Plus there's a purplish-yellow bruise forming above my collarbone.

I'm not sure where the hell that coulda come from.

I walk down the stairs and go into the kitchen, where my dad is drinking coffee. Sunlight streams in through the open window.

"Hey, what happened there?" my dad asks, noticing the bruise on my neck.

My hand goes to it reflexively. I pull my collar together to cover it. "I don't know," I say. "It's weird. I just—I woke up like this."

I pour myself coffee.

"You need to eat more iron," my dad says, handing me, somewhat incongruously, a box with some choco-late donuts in it.

I take one and do my best to smile.

"Not a lot of iron in these things."

"I'll get some steaks for dinner and . . . uh . . . maybe some broccoli?"

"That'd be nice," I say. "Thank you."

I eat the donut and drink coffee and my dad starts talking to me about the daily chores. Really, it's not so bad. Just a lot of dusting and straightening and organizing. No milking the cows or tilling the soil or whatever.

Worse than the chores are the hours of religious study my dad's planning to do with me. Homeschooling, he calls it. But my dad's not a big fan of Darwin. And his concept of history is a little . . . *skewed.* I'm not sure I'm gonna get through it without him killing me, or maybe the other way around.

But, for the moment anyway, I don't really care. The Percocet is doing its thing. The pain in my head is gone, replaced by a feeling of weightlessness, like cotton candy wrapped around my brain—in a good way.

I mean, *very* good.

Even my dad looks a little more . . . pleasant than he normally does.

Back in Johnstown I went to parties and stuff and would drink a little. But I've always been kind of scared of drinking too much. I never wanted to end up like my mom.

But one Percocet's not gonna kill me. And it turns

out it's making this day a whole lot more tolerable. So I finish the donut and coffee and decide I might as well just keep my pajamas on while I'm dusting and straightening around the house. I go upstairs and get my Discman so I can listen to music while I work. Marc Bolan singing "Cosmic Dancer."

"I danced myself into the tomb."

I dust along the railings and bookshelves and every picture frame and light fixture and curtain rod and spare piece of furniture. The dust is like half an inch thick in places—gray and greasy, filling my lungs so I cough and sneeze and my eyes burn. Eventually I have to tie a bandana over my nose and mouth.

I make my way through the front room and the dining room and the living room and the sitting room and the back study. The sun is warm coming in through the windows. I dust around the fireplace and around the doorframe and along the complicated floral-patterned wallpaper.

At the back of the house there is another locked room like the one upstairs, but my dad gave me the skeleton key to use, so I fit it in the lock and turn the handle. A cloud of dust envelops me and I cough and sneeze until it clears.

The room is dark and I smell that smell like mold

and decay. I stumble through the clutter and push open the back windows and take big, gasping breaths of the cool morning air. A wind blows through the branches of the dense forest. The stiff brown leaves are falling—carpeting the ground in a thick blanket.

Inside the room, white sheets are draped over more stored lamps and spare furniture and books and wooden frames and candlesticks.

I pull back one of the cloths and notice a small wooden box, inlaid with silver crosses, sitting atop a very old-looking table.

I open the box carefully and take out a man's gold ring that stands out against the black velvet lining. I hold it up to the light. A golden snake is coiled around a glittering ruby apple. I take the cold metal in my hand and turn it over. With Marc Bolan now singing, *"Girl, I'm just a vampire for your love."*

I drop the ring in my pocket.

I pull off another of the draped cloths and reveal a dark wood chest of drawers. There's a black-and-white photograph on top of it, a man and woman dressed in tailored suits and hats—like from the thirties or forties. The woman holds a swaddled infant in her arms and the man holds the hand of what I think is a young boy in a wool sweater. I open the top drawer and find a stack of similar photographs.

Alex's stories echo through my head. A home for wayward girls. Are these the couples who adopted the children born at Harmony House?

I don't know what other explanation there could be.

I keep on looking through the photographs, but then a sudden movement catches my attention. I turn to the window and see a figure crossing through the grass and then disappearing behind the line of trees. I go and lean out. A scrub jay screams loud from the treetops. Crows circle aimlessly overhead.

And then I see him.

That boy Colin.

He's crossing through the forest, I guess taking that path to the beach.

I drop down onto the grass and run fast to the covering of forest so my dad doesn't see me from the house. It must be the Percocet that gives me the courage, because I do it without even thinking.

Colin's back is to me. He's dressed in a big army jacket with the hood pulled up over his head. He's carrying a white bucket—like a painter's—by the handle, so it swings back and forth as he walks.

I want to catch up to him.

I stumble over the roots and low-hanging branches and the piles of wet, rotting leaves. It's cold in the forest—colder than it should be—and I shiver and wrap my arms tight around my body.

"Hey," I call out. "Hey, wait up."

Colin turns like I startled him.

"Jesus," he says. "You scared me."

I laugh. "I'm the least scary thing in a five-mile radius. Didn't you hear me flailing around back here?"

He laughs then, too.

"No, too deep in my own head, I guess." He glances down. "Are you wearing . . . slippers?"

I stare at my feet and realize he is, of course, right.

"Yeah, uh, I just saw you going past and I . . . wanted to talk to you. Are you heading to the beach?"

He nods.

"Uh-huh. It's low tide. I was gonna go see if I could get some oysters off the rocks."

"Oh, cool. You can do that here?"

"I do—almost every day."

"Can you eat them?"

"Yeah, of course. I'd ask you to come with me, only I'd say you need some better shoes. And maybe a jacket.

It gets crazy cold down by the surf."

"Yeah," I say, smiling. "Thanks, but I can't anyway. I'm supposed to be cleaning the house right now. Then my dad is, uh, *homeschooling* me later."

"Homeschooling?"

"Yeah, I'm one of those freaks now," I say. "It sucks. Or, uh, it's going to. We haven't actually started yet."

"Why don't you just go to high school in town?"

I shake my head. "It's a long story."

He grins. "I have time."

"I've gotta get back. I was gonna try to go into town later, though, if you wanted to maybe go to that diner with me and get some . . . coffee? Or something?"

He smiles more.

"I can't tonight," he says. "But maybe tomorrow? What about in the afternoon? We could go down to the beach?"

I smile, too.

"All right, yeah. That'd be great."

"Around two?" he asks.

I nod.

"Perfect."

"And . . . uh . . . be sure to wear some real shoes," he says.

I tell him I'll see him tomorrow.

I run back to the house.

I pull myself up and back in through the same window I used before—locking it shut behind me. Then I go back out into the hall and lock the storage room, too. The standing grandfather clock chimes ten times, over and over—low and resonating.

Ten a.m. I count it out loud.

That means I have two more hours of cleaning before lunch and then my dad's stupid lessons.

I put my headphones back on.

Marc Bolan sings, *"Life's a gas."*

Obviously, he never had to come to Harmony House.

After listening to *Electric Warrior* in its entirety, I move on to *The Slider*, and then Bowie's *Aladdin Sane*, and then finally, after lunch, it's time for my first day of homeschooling. My dad sits me down at the kitchen table and we go over Bible verses for a long, long time. Then we practice some algebra problems.

I actually kind of like it, believe it or not. Doing problems . . . I don't know . . . there's something fun about it—like playing a game. My dad doesn't really know shit about math, so all he can do is give me workbooks to get through. It's a good excuse to get out of here for a while.

What I ask him is, "Hey, Dad, can I take this math work into town? I noticed a little diner when we drove in. Maybe I could pick us up some dinner from there, bring it back? Do these problems while I wait? Then you won't have to go to the store or cook anything."

My dad nods slowly, scratching at his jawline. His thick fingernails are chewed down so they're bleeding in places.

"Yes," he says. "Yes, that's a good idea."

He lets his shoulders rise and fall. I play, absently, with the ring in my pocket.

"I gotta go change," I say.

My dad catches my wrist in his rough hand.

"What've you got there?" he asks.

"N-nothing," I say.

He takes the ring from out of my pocket and holds it up, staring. He grits his teeth together. His face flushes bright red.

"Where did you get this?" he almost yells.

"Oh, uh . . . I found it. It was in a back room."

My dad takes the ring and puts it in his own pocket. "Don't take things that aren't yours," he says.

He shakes his head.

Then he laughs.

"It's okay," he says. "Anyway, I'll take a BLT."

I blink. "What?"

"From the diner."

My dad is a psycho, I think. But obviously I don't say that out loud. What I do say is, "Sure."

"With French fries."

"Okay."

"But I mean it," he says. "There are things in this house. They're not . . . to be played with. Do you understand?"

"I do."

I run upstairs quickly and change—noticing that black devotional book laid open on my bed to the page where my mother's name is written out in delicate cursive letters.

It's strange—I don't remember leaving it here.

I pick it up off the floral bedspread and flip through the pages, feeling a knotting in my stomach.

For the first time I see that some of the words have been crossed out, as though with a black Magic Marker.

I turn to the Prayer of Saint Francis—

Lord, make me an instrument of Your

~~peace~~

Where there is hatred, let me sow ~~love~~
Where there is injury, pardon
Where there is discord, harmony
Where there is error, truth
Where there is doubt, faith
Where there is despair, ~~hope~~
Where there is darkness, light
And where there is sadness, joy.
O Divine Master, grant that I may not
   so much seek
To be consoled as to console
To be understood as to understand
To be loved as to ~~love~~.
For it is in giving that we receive
It is in pardoning that we are pardoned
And it is in dying that we are born to
   eternal ~~life~~.

I shiver.

It couldn't've been that way before. I mean, I would've seen it.

Could my dad have done it? That doesn't make any sense. Maybe he's trying to send some sort of message.

I wonder, then, if he's been looking through my

things. It's the only explanation.

I drop the book on the floor and pull back the sheets and comforter on the bed. I reach my hand under the pillow, where I left the photograph of my mother.

My breath catches. It's not there.

I throw the pillows off the bed and pull the bed frame back from the wall, to see if maybe it fell, but I can't find it anywhere.

"Motherfucker!" I say out loud.

Then I run to the closet and feel in the lining of my coat for where I left that bag of pills. Thank God they're still there, at least.

But why would my dad take my mom's picture?

There's a high-pitched whining creak of a floorboard behind me and I turn, startled, feeling someone's eyes on me.

"Dad, what the—"

But as I spin around, there's no one there.

Helplessly, I decide to take another Percocet to calm down. My mind is really fucking with me. Sweat beads on my forehead and my shirt clings to my back. But I'm still cold and . . . again . . . I shiver. I put on my jacket and a pair of black boots and sling my backpack over one shoulder.

I go down the stairs—hurrying past the second floor and my dad's room.

I go out into the coming dark.

The walk into town is long and I listen to another Bowie CD, *The Rise and Fall of Ziggy Stardust and the Spiders from Mars*. A few cars drive slowly past.

By the time I get to the diner the sun has set almost completely and a cold wind blows discarded trash and newspapers up the mostly empty street. I push the swinging glass door open to the warm, brightly lit diner, where the smell of coffee and baking pies makes me suddenly very hungry.

There are already a few older people inside, hunched over tables and drinking coffee at the counter. For the first time I notice a framed poster of Patsy Cline, live at Carnegie Hall, hung up on one of the white, pristine painted walls.

At a corner table, Christy is there with two girls sitting in front of, but not eating, a plate of French fries.

Aunt Rose sees me first. She's chopping a big stack of carrots with her back to me, but turns when the door dings open and smiles.

"Jen! Hey, how are you?"

And then to Christy, "Chris, you see Jen is here?"

I raise my hand meekly to say hello.

Christy gets up and bounds over to me, surprising me with a hug. She's wearing an orange-and-white down vest over a turtleneck, and her blond hair is tied tight in a high ponytail.

"Hey! Come and meet my friends!" she says. Before I can argue she takes my hand in hers and leads me, still bouncing, back to her corner table.

A girl she introduces as Candace is around our age, very pretty, with dark skin and a weave cut shoulder-length with bangs. The other girl, Mercedes, looks maybe a little older. She has long black hair and pale skin with the etchings of dark circles under her large brown eyes. We all wave stupidly at each other and I sit next to Candace, across from Christy and Mercedes—who I notice is wearing a Joy Division T-shirt.

"Were you guys all at school today?" I ask.

"Yeah," says Candace. "One more day 'til the weekend."

"Thank Christ," says Mercedes.

Rose comes over and takes my order, which is coffee and eggs and bacon and toast. They serve breakfast all day. It's not a bad place, I think.

"Jen's the one I told you about," says Christy. "The one who's living at Harmony House for the winter."

"Whoa," says Candace.

"Creepy," says Mercedes.

They both laugh.

I do not.

Instead, I put sugar and milk in my coffee.

"How's it going so far?" asks Christy.

I tell her it's okay, I guess.

"What's the house like?" Mercedes asks. "I've never been up there."

I let my shoulders rise and fall. I drink some coffee and spin the cup around absently in my hands.

"I don't know," I say, feeling awkward suddenly.

"What I heard," Candace says, "is it used to be like a house for unwed mothers—run by like nuns, or something. And I heard the monsignor guy, you know, who ran the place, used to torture those girls. Like he used to do all these terrible things to them."

"Terrible things like what?" I ask.

The three girls all look at one another. Finally, Christy says, very quietly, "Those are just rumors." She puts a delicate hand on mine, halting the endless turning of the coffee mug.

"No, it's okay," I say. "I don't mind."

"You know what else I heard?" Candace says. "That the guy who built the house back in the 1800s killed his wife and daughter."

"No," says Mercedes. "I heard it was the daughter that killed her mom and dad."

Christy shakes her head. "I'm pretty sure the daughter just killed herself. Then the mom killed herself, too. And the dad went crazy. That's what Rose told me."

"Nice," I say. "So, basically, I'm staying at the Overlook Hotel."

They laugh.

"I think it's cool you're staying there," says Candace. "I'm impressed."

"Well," I say. "You guys can come over. Anytime. Is there a video store in town?"

"They rent 'em at the deli," says Christy. "Maybe we could get some scary movies and sleep over."

"I'd like that," I say, meaning it. "Tomorrow night, maybe?"

The girls look at each other again, then nod and smile.

"Sure, that'd be great," says Christy.

I smile now, too.

"Perfect," I say.

We go on talking like that for a while and, I guess not surprisingly, I don't end up doing any math homework. I eat the eggs and bacon and toast and then order a BLT and French fries for my dad.

I say good-bye to the girls and to Rose and decide to cut over to the deli, real quick, to rent some videos before going home.

Again not surprisingly, the selection of videos at the deli pretty much sucks. But I end up renting *The Omen* with Gregory Peck, a movie with Donald Sutherland called *Don't Look Now*, which I've never seen, John Carpenter's *The Thing*, *The Devil Rides Out*, and *The Silence of the Lambs*, in case the girls haven't seen it, though they probably have. By the time I leave the deli, I'm pretty well weighed down with bags of videos, candy, and all the food from the Double R.

Out on the street the wind has picked up and I feel chilled all over as I walk back toward the house.

Thankfully, I've only been walking for about half a block when that girl Candace drives by in a silver Volkswagen Jetta. She rolls the passenger window down and tells me to get in.

"Thank you so much," I say, stepping off the curb.

A voice calls from behind me. My breath catches and my stomach goes tight. I turn back to see Alex walking out of the shadows.

"Hey," he calls out. "Where you think you're going?"

I stand staring at him for a minute.

"Yo, Alex, get fucked!" Candace yells, flipping him off.

"Come on," she tells me. "Come on, get in."

Alex is looking directly at me, his eyes black and vacant.

"Come on," says Candace again.

I climb quickly into the car.

Alex watches us go.

"What was that about?" Candace asks, taking out a cigarette from a pack of Parliaments and offering me one.

I take it and thank her and use her lighter to light it, my hands shaking kind of bad.

"He just wouldn't leave me alone yesterday," I say, not wanting to make too big a deal out of it. "I don't know what the hell is wrong with that guy."

I inhale and exhale.

Candace shakes her head. "He's an asshole."

"Seriously."

Candace drives me up the twisting driveway to Harmony House. She stops the car, stares up at the house a moment, her eyes wary.

"Don't worry," she tells me, her gaze fixed on the dark face of Harmony House. "Everything's gonna be okay."

I thank her for the ride.

And I hope to God she's right.

CHAPTER 5

When I tell my dad about the girls at the diner and our plans for a sleepover, he agrees to let them come over so long as I do all my work and pray and am a good girl. Of course, I agree. I'll tell him anything he wants to hear so long as I don't have to be trapped here with him by myself all the time.

After he eats dinner, he makes me pray again with him up in his room. He kneels with me on the floor and grasps his long, bony hands together.

I submit to this for as long as I have to.

And then I go back downstairs to watch the super-weird Donald Sutherland, Nicolas Roeg dwarf lady serial killer movie.

When it's over I go upstairs and brush my teeth and then go back to my ugly-ass pink room.

On the floor, where I left it, that book of Bible verses is open to that same page with the Prayer of Saint Francis of Assisi on it. Only now, I mean, unless I really am going fucking crazy, it looks like there are even more words crossed out. I can't understand it. I pick the book up off the floor and read the prayer again.

> *Lord, make me an instrument of Your*
> *~~peace~~*
> *Where there is hatred, let me sow ~~love~~*
> *Where there is injury, pardon*
> *Where there is discord, harmony*
> *Where there is error, truth*
> *Where there is doubt, ~~faith~~*
> *Where there is despair, ~~hope~~*
> *Where there is darkness, light*
> *And where there is sadness, joy.*
> *O Divine Master, grant that I may not*
> *so much seek*

To be ~~consoled~~ *as to* ~~console~~
To be understood as to understand
To be loved as to ~~love~~.
For it is in giving that we receive
It is in pardoning that we are pardoned
And it is in dying that we are born to
     eternal ~~life~~.

Jesus Christ, I think, I'm really fucking losing it.

I go to the closet and get out another one of the pills from the baggie in my jacket lining. This one, I think, is a Xanax. I dry-swallow it and then take some deep breaths and try to relax.

Somehow the window has been left open. The night air is cold and smells strongly of pine needles and the distant ocean. Leaning my body halfway out, I can see the stars clearly now—bright and compli-cated, glittering in the dark, like a child's drawing of what the night sky looks like. The wind has died, so there is only the cold and the sounds of crickets and rustling of raccoons or maybe deer in the forest below. I hear what I think might be a horse whinnying not far away. I wonder, then, if that gray cat has found a home for the night, though I'm sure it must belong to one of the neighboring houses.

I decide to bring it in the house and give it some milk if I see it again tomorrow.

Then I turn off the light and go climb into the unfamiliar bed, under unfamiliar sheets and blankets, with unfamiliar smells all around me.

My eyes start to close and I hear someone whisper . . . *"Good night."*

It's my mother's voice, but I'm too tired to care.

It's all in my mind, I tell myself, anyway.

And I start to drift off.

And in the coming of sleep, I have a strange dream— or a strange vision.

It enters my brain like a long nail being driven in deeper and deeper and then deeper still.

The pain is searing.

But I don't resist it.

I see:

At a dining room table—set with fine china and crystal glasses, a silver candelabra hung with glittering jewels, and a centerpiece of red and yellow dahlias—a family sits rigidly in their straight-backed chairs. They do not speak.

The little girl, no more than seven or eight years of

age, wears a white dress trimmed with lace and black ankle boots. Her inky black hair is combed back behind her ears, which stick out a little on either side. A silver-and-pearl brooch is pinned to her chest. As she picks up her glass to drink, her vivid blue eyes catch the light. Her pupils reflect the candle's flame.

Next to the girl, at the head of the table, her father sits eating with perfect poise and delicacy. He cuts his lamb into tiny pieces and chews the meat slowly and deliberately. He has a broad face with burning blue eyes like his daughter's. His nose is sharp and angular.

Across from the little girl, her mother sits drinking wine from a crystal glass, the fine lines around her small mouth like a wood etching.

Rain falls against the windows.

The sound like static.

At the table, the father puts down his fork and knife, then takes a drink from his burgundy-colored wine. "Why, do you know that today I received a letter from General Grant himself?"

He turns to look at his daughter. She freezes. A wan smile spreads across the father's face, his teeth white, but crooked. Beneath the table, he puts his hand on his daughter's knee.

"You all right, dear?"

His hand tightens on her.

Her breath catches.

Sweat breaks out on her forehead.

She shivers.

Her mother averts her eyes.

The girl holds her breath.

And then her father removes his hand.

He returns to his plate.

And the girl's legs begin to shake.

A thud hits the floor at the foot of my bed, tearing me out of the strange dream. I gasp and sit up, alert suddenly, scrambling to turn on the bedside lamp.

"Who's there?" I say.

I grab the covers up all around me and blink my eyes.

Someone is moving through the room.

From off the floor the figure rises up—big, swaying arms stretched out toward me.

His blond-brown hair is sticking up, matted on one side—his eyes unfocused. He rocks back and forth.

"This place looks different from last time," he says, strangely calm.

It's Alex.

He stares at me with those glazed eyes, jaw slack, for what feels like a very long time.

Then he bends down in my face. I can smell the alcohol on his breath.

"Now, you listen to me. You listen like a good little girl."

He grabs my arm tight as I try to move away.

"I tried to be good to you. And now you're going to be nice to me. You're going to be nice—"

My heart beats loud in my ears. Fast—before I can move—he climbs onto the bed, his legs pinning me down.

"Stop! Stop it," I say, my voice finally working.

He grabs at my hair. Holds it tight in his fist, then shifts his weight to press his stinking lips on mine, but there is enough room for me to knee him between his legs.

"Fuck you!" I say now, the words clear and forceful. I feel a strength rising up from the very center of me like a fire catching and consuming my body, and I knee him hard between the legs.

He groans and clutches himself and rolls off the bed.

I bolt from the room and run out into the hall.

"DAD!" I scream. "DAD! DAD! HELP!"

But then Alex is there, limping up behind me, clutching his stomach—coming on fast.

I scream louder, "DAD!"

I sprint to the stairs, hearing Alex's strained breathing, his heavy footsteps.

"DAD!"

I run down the stairs, tripping and almost falling, but catching myself on the banister.

"DAD!"

I stumble and run from room to room, opening and closing doors—lost—hearing Alex's heavy footsteps and breathing right behind me. As I run along the hallway again I hear a voice whispering just behind me, *"Jump."* But I keep running and running and I don't fucking stop.

That portrait, the one my dad said looks like me, catches the moonlight in a way that makes the girl's eyes appear all black and like her mouth is turned upward in a mocking smile. The sight of it makes me stop for a second—like I've become somehow frozen in her vacant stare. Alex, too, seems to stop—just as transfixed by the strange painting as I am.

But then another voice whispers in my ear—the

voice like my mother's. *"Run,"* it says. *"Run."*

And so I do run—taking the stairs two and three at a time—until we reach the bottom floor and my foot catches on the rug. I call out as I fall and turn to see Alex bearing down on me.

I try to get to my feet and sprint away from him again, but instead slam into the big wooden dresser. From up top something teeters and comes crashing down. Alex shrieks like an animal caught in a trap. He drops on his knees and howls and clutches at his face.

A light switches on overhead. I blink my eyes, trying to focus on the crumpled mass at my feet.

My father's voice comes echoing down the corridor. "Jen? Jen? What's happening? What's wrong?"

"I . . . I'm over here," I call out.

On the floor, next to Alex, I see a crumpled picture of my mother sticking out of a broken frame. In the photo my mother is smiling, holding an infant me in her arms.

"Jen?" my dad yells.

I look from the picture to Alex there, writhing on the floor. He moves his hands away from his face—a spurt of blood sprays out from the corner of his eye. Big shards of glass from the broken frame are sticking out of his huge, white face. The blood runs down wet and glossy.

"Jen," my dad says, coming up behind me.

I don't turn around.

I stay looking down at Alex, as he looks up at me.

He opens his mouth—a greasy-looking, bright red-colored bubble of blood forms on his lips.

His mouth opens wider.

The bubble pops.

CHAPTER 6

Alex remains unconscious on the floor and my father paces over him.

I sit facing away from my dad and Alex lying unconscious on the floor, pulling an afghan tighter around my shoulders.

I stare into the gaping fireplace, remembering my mother. I can see the two of us at the public pool.

It's hot.

The kind of heat that makes your skin itch.

But the water is cold and feels good as I plunge

beneath it, holding my breath. I've been playing in the shallow end of the pool for hours.

My mom lies on the hard plastic lounge chair. She reads her book, wearing big sunglasses and a straw hat.

She calls me out to apply more sunscreen.

I do as she says, climbing out of the water and standing drying in the sun. I sigh and fidget while she rubs the lotion all over me. It's light pink and thick and has a faint powdery scent that tickles my nose.

"My poor pale princess," she says. "But you're so fair, you'll burn right up."

She laughs.

"Hurry up, Mom," I say.

"Almost finished and . . . there!"

I sprint for the water's edge, about to dive.

"Jennifer! Jennifer, wait!" my mother yells.

But I don't stop.

I jump high.

But in midair, I feel a powerful shove to the side.

I miss the pool entirely, landing splayed on the hard concrete.

I yelp, and when I look down I see my leg and part of my hand are scraped and bloody. I let out a cry of pain and my mother rushes up to me.

"Jen, oh my gosh, are you okay?"

The lifeguard is with us now. She leans over, asking if anything is broken, if we need any help.

"Someone pushed me," I cry, embarrassed.

My mother wraps her arms around me. She talks over me. "Hush, baby. Hush, now. You're okay." She glances at the lifeguard. "She'll be fine. I can take it from here."

My mother leads me back to her chair.

"Don't ever run away from me like that again," she says.

"But, Mom, I—"

"You left your water wings," she says, turning to look at the inflated orange plastic water wings decorated with Rainbow Brite and her white unicorn.

"I'm sorry," she says.

She hugs me to her.

"You don't know how to swim yet. Don't ever, *ever* go in the water without your water wings again. Do you understand me?"

I stare into her bright blue eyes.

And here, sitting by the empty fire, I think about that push in the air.

And the picture in the frame falling.

And then I don't want to think about it anymore.

CHAPTER 7

An ambulance from Stafford Township takes Alex away.

The county sheriff, Cody Jarrett—a silver-haired man with leathery skin, straight, block teeth, and a long, pointed chin—drinks our coffee and eats our donuts and smokes Pall Mall cigarettes while he takes down my statement in the living room. His eyes are a clouded, milky blue and he writes in a small legal pad, nodding his head absently as I tell and retell the story of what happened.

Sheriff Jarrett doesn't seem particularly surprised about any of it.

"Alex Winter's been a problem 'round this town pretty near since he could walk. I'm just sorry you had to run into him."

His voice is calm and deep, with an accent from maybe Georgia or the Carolinas.

He sits on one of the straight-backed chairs, crossing his legs and then uncrossing them again. I sit on the fold-out stepladder and cry a little and the sheriff tells me it's going to be all right. My dad stands behind me, looking down coolly at me. He keeps chewing on his bottom lip and there's this thick blue vein standing out in his forehead.

I find myself not wanting Sheriff Jarrett—and his deputy, a tall Native American guy named Coburn—to leave at the end of the interview.

But soon the sheriff is putting a hand on my shoulder, telling me not to worry, that he's going to make sure Alex Winter never bothers me again. I'll have to testify at the trial, he says—there's no way around that. But he'll do everything he can to keep me safe.

"You've been through enough already," he says. "I hope you can put this behind you." He promises to check up on me again in a few days.

To my dad he says, "You've got a very brave girl here, Mr. Noonan."

"Yes, well . . ."

They shake hands.

My dad walks the two officers out the front door and I go back up the stairs, closing my bedroom door and making sure the window is shut tight and locked. The light on the bedside table, with colonial figures embroidered into the dark-stained canvas lamp shade, reflects patterns on the pink pastel walls.

I swallow two more of the pills. Then I reach over and turn off the light just as my dad's heavy footsteps sound from the staircase. I pull the covers up. The door to my room opens and my dad stands there, beneath the dull orange glow from the hallway.

"Come on," he says through his clenched teeth. "We're going to pray."

I sit up in bed.

"What? Dad, please. I'm really tired. I just want to go to sleep."

He rubs his chin with his long fingers.

"No," he finally says. "No, you must pray. . . . We must ask God for forgiveness."

"What do you mean? What do I have to ask forgiveness for?" I ask, feeling the knot in my stomach turn to a kind of smoldering ash—like an ember catching and starting to burn, slowly.

"You know what I mean," he says. "You know exactly."

There's something in his eyes, the way the light hits them, that I don't think I've ever seen before. His gaunt features are pulled taut—straining in every direction—mouth turned down, eyes bulging, jaw clicking back and forth. His hair is plastered to his forehead with sweat and there's a smell like sickness coming off him.

"Dad," I say, the heat growing like a weed inside me. "What's wrong with you?"

He shakes his head.

"I want you to come pray with me," he says. "I want you to pray for forgiveness. I'll not let Him take you the way he took your mother. I failed with her. But I won't fail with you. I've received a vision, Jen. . . ."

I gather the blankets up around me as if, again, they might offer me some protection. "A vision?" I say. "What are you talking about?"

He steps forward into my room, his tall frame enveloped in the shadowy darkness.

"The devil was in your mother. And the devil is in you."

"Dad . . ."

"You're being tested. You are a prophet, Jen. And

all the prophets are tested."

"I'm a prophet?" I actually almost laugh at that. "Look, I think we both got pretty freaked out by what happened, but . . ."

"No," he says, cutting me off. "No, I see clearly. Coming here, to this house—I've seen God's will for me . . . and for you. He wants me to save you, the way I couldn't save your mother. He wants me to save you. And then you will go forth and tell the people. You will warn them of the terrible speed of God's mercy."

"Dad," I say, my voice cracking. "Dad, come on. You're not making any sense."

"I'm making sense," he says. "The only sense there is."

"But this wasn't my fault," I say.

He drops down on the bed next to me, the mattress and wooden frame sagging beneath his weight—though he remains rigidly straight, speaking as if to the room and its darkness.

"You're right," he says, sounding calmer now. "It was my fault. I should have prepared you better. But I will now. I will not stop until you have been saved—until you fulfill your destiny."

"Dad, please," I say. "I think we both need to get some sleep."

I see the silhouette of his head nodding up and down.

"Yes," he says. "But first we will pray. We will pray for your salvation. We will pray for your soul."

He takes hold of my arm with his damp, cloying hand and pulls me to the floor. The carpet feels rough through the light fabric of my pajamas. I want to cry suddenly or . . . I don't know what. I'm all flushed with shame and helplessness.

"Have mercy on us, O Lord," my dad says, his voice soft, but growing ever louder. "We are sinners and we know not what we do. Grant us the ability to see your fire and glory. Wash away our sins with your blood, O Lord. Cleanse us with your divine mercy. Take pity on us. The devil has my daughter held tightly in his hands, the way he had my wife. He wants her soul. He has lain with her. He has tempted her. And she cannot resist, Lord, without your strength and protection. Keep her from His terrible embrace, Lord. Help her to be ready, Lord, so that on the last day, she'll rise in your glory. Do not let her follow the path that her mother took. Help her to resist. Lead her not into eternal damnation. . . ."

Listening to his droning, beseeching, babbling voice, I notice the heat is mixed with a sickness rising from inside—crawling into every corner of my body, burning in my eyes. I want to scream and tear myself apart.

Tears run down my cheeks.

"Cleanse her soul, Lord," my dad says. "Let her choose righteousness over worldly pleasures. . . ."

I clench my fists tighter and tighter—my nails digging into the palms of my hands.

"Show her the light and love of our savior, Jesus Christ. . . ."

Finally, I can't take it anymore. The humiliation of kneeling here, listening to this . . . fucking crazy bullshit . . . overwhelms me and I want to scream, "Stop it! Stop it! Stop it!"

But instead, there is a loud pop of surging electricity. The bulb from the hallway flashes bright white and then extinguishes in an instant.

The entire house appears drowning in darkness.

"I think the power went out," I say, choking back all the rage and hatred I have for him at this moment.

"Probably a circuit breaker," he says calmly. "I saw a flashlight under the sink. I'll go take a look."

His voice has lost its thick-tongued, frenzied slurring. He sounds again like he normally does—which is crazy, but not that fucking bat-shit crazy.

"You go to sleep now," he says. "Try and get some rest."

He gets up off the floor and, just as suddenly as he walked in here, he walks out. I hear his footsteps shuffling carefully down the hall and then, slowly, down the stairs. There is no light coming from anywhere.

Exhausted and weak-feeling, I curl on the floor, crying silently.

All the heat inside me has drained out to nothing and I shiver there. I almost don't have the strength to pull myself back up into bed.

But I do.

I climb into bed and shiver beneath the covers.

I think, then, that if only he could've been the one to die—my dad, and not her—if he'd been the one to choke to death on his own vomit—with a blood alcohol level of 3.6—then everything would be better.

I think that and then I wish him dead.

I pray for it.

That's one thing I actually do pray for.

I pray for him to die and I pray wishing my mother was back with me.

I pray like that until I fall asleep.

And in sleep, maybe as an answer to my prayer, I dream of my mother.

She's standing in our old kitchen, her black hair cut short—bangs over her eyes—drinking black liquid out of a whiskey glass. The kitchen table looms above me, casting long shadows, like I'm sitting on the floor looking up.

My mom drinks the drink and it spills down her chin and onto the men's dress shirt she's wearing. The black is thick like motor oil. It covers her body—it spreads across the floor.

"Mom!" I call. "Mom!"

But no sound comes out.

"Mom!"

She can't hear me.

"Mom!"

I'm choking on my own voice.

When I turn I see my dad standing in the doorway, facing away from me.

I call out to him then, too, but he will not turn around.

"Dad!"

The table rocks back and forth above me. It rocks from one side to the other, threatening to come crashing down at any second.

"It's going to fall!" I yell.

But, of course, no one hears me.

The table hits the floor and the tile cracks in two and the whole house begins to break apart around me.

I scream so loud I scream myself clear out of the dream and into the gray, pale early-morning light.

The sun is just the faintest flicker on the horizon. I pull the covers up and tuck my legs in, curling as tight as possible.

And then I fall back asleep.

And again, I dream.

CHAPTER 8

When my dad knocks on the door it takes me several seconds before I realize where I am. The sun is low over the horizon, but pain cuts through the center of my forehead and makes it difficult to open my eyes. The sound of my dad's fist against the heavy door is like a drill bit against my skull—breaking through into the soft tissue of my brain.

"Just a second," I say, trying to sit up.

The room spins around me and my head aches and my stomach turns.

I vomit into the wastebasket by my bed.

"What's going on?" my dad calls, pushing the door open. "Are you sick?"

"Uh, no . . . I feel great," I say, and then vomit again.

Out of the corner of my eye I see my dad nodding.

"Our prayers are working. Your body is cleansing itself," he says, "ridding itself of evil. Why don't you try fasting today? I'll do it with you."

"Right now," I say, gasping for breath, "fasting isn't gonna be a problem."

"I had another vision last night," my dad says. "The Lord spoke to me. The plan I have is the right one. He has great things in store for us."

"I'm really not feeling well," I tell him.

"We must pray together," he says.

I try to sit up again and, this time, the room keeps more or less still for me.

"Fine," I say. "Fine. Let me just get cleaned up a little."

My dad comes over and takes the wastebasket full of puke from off the floor.

"I'll take care of this," he says. "Get dressed and come down."

"Okay," I say—too weak to fight with him anymore.

He walks out of the room and I push myself up and

squint my eyes against the sun coming in too bright.

"Hey," I yell, remembering suddenly. "Is the power back on?"

My dad shouts back from the top of the stairs.

"It was a circuit breaker. Just like I said."

So he was right about one thing, I guess.

I walk staggering over to the closet. After last night I feel like I need to take ten thousand of those pills from Stephanie's dad. But I only take one. I dry-swallow it down and then go to the bathroom and drink water from the tap and wash my face and brush my teeth—twice—to try to get the awful taste of bile out of my mouth.

The sickness and nausea in me is replaced by an intense hunger. I hold my stomach—hands shaking—dizzy and aching. There's a vacuous pit opening up inside me that feels like it can never possibly be filled. The pain of the hunger shoots up and down my body and across from shoulder to shoulder.

Moving as quietly as I can, so my dad doesn't hear me, I make my way down the stairs. But it does no good. My dad comes out in the hall and calls out to me.

"Jen, where are you going? We have to pray together."

"Dad, I'm so hungry," I tell him, almost whimpering.

"Please, I've been sick. I have to eat."

"We're going to fast today," he answers back. "You can't give in to earthly temptation. The Lord will give you the food of life; you don't need anything else."

"Yes, I do," I tell him. "I need to eat. I have to."

The sickness tears at my stomach. It climbs up my throat. I feel my tongue swollen. Sweat beads on my forehead. My legs are weak beneath me and I grab the banister and my dad yells, "You mind me now!"

"I can't," I say. "I'm sick. Really."

"God wants you to repent," he says.

He starts toward me.

"No," I say. "No."

And then from above us a shrill, grating, high-pitched bleating makes me cover my ears. I look up to see the red LED light of the smoke detector flashing over and over—the sound bone-penetrating, like metal trying to cut metal. I set my teeth and call out loud, "I can't deal with this!"

The curtain starts to come down again and my head swims and I hurry down the rest of the stairs—away from the noise—not waiting for him to say anything else.

In the kitchen, the sun coming in through the narrow windows offers no warmth at all. My bare feet are cold on the tile and I shiver and feel the aching in my stomach. The sound of the smoke detector going off is distant now and faint and when I close the kitchen door I can hear it only as a steady, pulsing rhythm like a too-rapid heartbeat.

I breathe out and try to figure out what to eat—still not sure what my body can handle. I decide to just put some toast in the toaster and boil water for tea. The hunger in me is combined with a terrible, unquenchable thirst now. The more water I drink, the more the thirst clings to my throat like I'm swallowing the desert.

I glance up at the clock then, waiting for the toast to toast and the water to boil. I wonder how long it's been since I took that pill. I need the relief it promises me so badly now.

"Jen," I hear my dad calling—the sound of the smoke detector now gone completely. "Come on. It's fixed."

I'm too weak and exhausted to call back. The hunger cramps my stomach and the thirst parches my tongue.

But when the toast finally does pop and I spread butter on it and try to eat, I find the sweeping nausea is too much for me again. What little I get down comes right back up again. I'm so frustrated and sick I bang my fist against the counter.

I sit down in one of the straight-backed chairs at the breakfast table and close my eyes. I wait, counting the seconds.

Finally, the cold in me begins to thaw. The pain and aching subsides. I feel a flood of beautiful warmth and weightlessness as whatever that pill was works its way into my bloodstream. I breathe out. And then I can eat. I take small bites, chewing the bits of toast well and swallowing them easily. I drink black tea with milk and no sugar.

"Thank God," I say aloud.

But I'm not delivered yet.

My dad comes marching into the kitchen, his jaw held tight in anger—his ashen skin gone red in the face.

"I told you to hurry up," he says. "You think this is a joke? I'm talking about your soul here. Your soul—your chance at salvation."

I don't let him see me roll my eyes.

But I'm too blissed out to argue with him. The path of least resistance is to follow him up the stairs. And the greatest thing about whatever that pill was is that it's given me the freedom just not to care—and that is the greatest freedom of all.

When I do get to his room, though, the smell of

mold and something rotting makes me recoil, the dank, fetid air thick in my lungs.

Immediately, I go over to the window and start to open it, but my dad tells me to leave it as it is.

"Come kneel with me," he says.

I turn away from the window, looking up at the bleeding Jesus on the cross—the crown of thorns cutting in—the nails piercing his flesh. There's a dresser painted a pale blue beneath the cross and on it my dad has lit a number of different-colored dripping candles. In the center of the candles is a beaded rosary and a small framed painting of the Virgin Mary.

I kneel down next to my dad.

He speaks the prayer out loud and grips his hands tightly together so I can see his protruding knuckles turning white. His hands tremble slightly. He asks God to show me the light of his love and grant my soul's salvation. He prays for my place in the kingdom of Heaven alongside his. He asks for mercy. He asks for forgiveness. He asks for guidance. He affirms the power and glory of the Lord.

I close my eyes and open them and feel deeply tired suddenly—but in a pleasant way so I almost drift off, my dad's voice droning on and on.

But through my nodding out I catch a glimpse of something out of the corner of my eye that suddenly shocks me wide-awake, and almost instantly sober—at least, seemingly so.

On the dresser with the candles and the rosary and the Virgin Mary, beneath Christ and the cross, is that ring—the one I found—the one my dad took from me. It's been placed in the shadow behind the framed painting, but as the candle flickers I can see the light reflecting off the image of the coiled serpent embossed in gold.

The sight of the ring makes me feel chilled. I shiver from somewhere very deep inside me. But my dad doesn't take any notice. He keeps on praying with his eyes closed and his hands clasped together.

I look at him, then, studying the newly formed lines and creases in his hollowed-out face. I notice that his hair seems to be thinning on top—even more so than yesterday, if that's possible. And the veins along his temples and cutting down the middle of his forehead are protruding like a tangle of branches beneath his scaly, sallow skin.

Could it be that my mom's death is finally catching up with him, I wonder—that he's finally letting himself feel it? Or is it what happened last night to me?

I close my eyes and keep them closed. I can't stand to look at him anymore.

Finally, though, he finishes the prayer.

He gets up and I see now that there are tears running down his face. He turns away from me.

The sun has risen higher up over the trees and is projecting the littlest bit of warmth in through the glass.

"You may go now," he tells me.

The sun has risen higher up over the trees and is projecting the littlest bit of warmth in through the glass.

"You may go now," he tells me.

I stand, feeling lightheaded. I step out into the hall—the walls collapsing in around me—a slide projector click, clicking in my brain—showing me images as though in sleep, but I am awake now.

I see the pretty nun. She sits on the grass beneath one of the live oaks in the back of Harmony House with the same little boy that was in her room. He wears blue wool shorts and a white, short-sleeved button-down shirt. He eats bread and cheese and the sister eats an apple. They work together on his catechism lessons. Wasps gather in the branches overhead— the steady droning buzz like an engine revving over and over.

"Okay, is the likeness in the body or the soul?" the young sister asks, putting a hand gently on the boy's shoulder.

The boy shakes his head.

"I don't know," he says.

She smiles.

"Come on, yes, you do."

The boy shakes his head again, eyes wide and glinting in the hot, bright sun, watching her lovingly—staring. The light casts shadows through the myriad colored leaves. A red-shouldered hawk cries hoarsely and dives down over the tall grass. A gray cat runs out from under the back porch steps and goes chasing after the low-flying bird.

But the boy remains fixed on the pretty young sister.

"I want to run away from here," the boy says. "I want you to come with me. I want to run away together."

The sister laughs.

"Because you don't like your catechism work?"

"Because I don't like Sister Angelica. Or monsignor."

The sister glances quickly around and tells the boy to hush.

"You can't say that," she says.

The boy bites on his thumbnail.

"I don't care," he says. "I want to go away with you. We could go to the moon together and be happy there."

Now the sister laughs again.

"The moon? How would we live on the moon?"

"We could grow vegetables," the boy says, very earnestly. "We could bring a cow . . . and chickens . . . and you could read me stories . . . and I could make a fire at night."

"That sounds nice," the sister says. "Just you and me . . . on the moon."

"You won't ever leave me?" the boy asks.

The sister hugs him to her.

"Never."

She takes a striped rubber ball up from next to the catechism book.

"Should we take a little break?" she asks. "You want to play catch?"

The boy jumps to his feet happily. She tosses him the ball and he runs down the sloping hill to the edge of the forest. The sister throws him the ball back, but it hits the ground and goes bouncing off at a right angle, disappearing into the dense covering of trees. The boy laughs and calls out, "I'll get it." Then he trudges through the wet leaves and ferns, searching for the missing ball.

He walks deeper into the forest, following a shallow creek bed until he sees another sister in a habit. She stands next to a thickset man with a shapeless fedora and a wool flannel shirt and mud-caked work boots. The man leans his weight on a wood-handled shovel. His hands are giant, with wide tobacco-stained fingernails. The sister holds a bundle covered in coarse-looking cloth, her head bowed. The man and sister talk quietly back and forth. And the boy walks slowly forward—the ball now forgotten.

As the darkness of the forest envelops the boy more and more he hesitates, then stops, then looks behind him. The young, pretty sister is there now, holding her arm out to him.

"Come on," she says, her eyes wide—her hands trembling. "Come away from here."

The boy turns back to the man and the sister with the bundle. He takes another step forward.

"Come on, now," the young sister says. "Let's go. We can go to the moon."

The boy steps forward again.

The sister with the bundle turns toward the boy now. The coarse-looking cloth is pulled back to show the body of an infant, its face swollen and icy blue. The sister holds it in her arms. She sees the boy watching. She sees the young, pretty sister.

"Sister Margaret," the older nun snaps. "Get that child out of here."

The nun turns again toward the grave.

"Sister Margaret," the little boy cries.

He bursts into tears.

The name echoes through the cavernous woods.

"Sister Margaret, Sister Margaret."

She crouches in the ferns and wet leaves. The boy runs to her. She takes him up in her arms. And they emerge together—back out into the bright midday sun.

And then like all the visions before it, this one fades to nothing.

I shake my head.

I press the palms of my hands in to my temples.

"What the hell is wrong with you?" I say out loud.

It's like I'm having seizures.

Or like I'm falling asleep where I stand.

Am I some kind of narcoleptic?

Or is it the pills I'm taking?

I go on to do my chores.

Because thinking about it doesn't do a fuckin' thing.

So I walk through the house, and in the shafts of pale white pearly sunlight, I can see a thick layer of dust along the banister. It covers every doorframe and painting and ornamental table and lamp and bookshelf and chest of drawers. The dust seems to have rained down in the night—as though someone came and deliberately coated each and every surface.

It wasn't like this yesterday, I think. But, again, that doesn't make any goddamn sense.

Looking up as I make my way down the stairs, I see the beams of the house and crisscrossed rafters and detailed edges and ornamental fixtures all seeming to point in slightly different directions. I think back on what Colin told me—that every line of the house, every angle, was built just the littlest bit off, so nothing connects the way it should—or the way you'd expect it to—giving the impression that it's moving constantly, shifting, expanding and contracting like lungs breathing in and out.

It does almost feel like the house is alive. Not a conscious being, exactly. Like an amoeba—a single-celled organism.

Still dusting and straightening as I go, I walk through the cluttered living room—past the armoire I crashed into last night—and as I do, I feel the life in the house traveling from corner to corner, following me from room to room, watching me wherever I go. I turn a corner, clicking off the last room's light.

At the end of the hall the locked room is standing open. There's no key in the lock, but the door is thrown wide.

"Dad, are you in there?"

I shiver, stepping inside, my hand still covering my nose, breathing only through my mouth.

The dust is deeper here and cloying and the smell of mold and rot makes me recoil back.

"Dad?" I call again.

I flick the light switch on, but nothing happens.

I try again.

The room stays dark. I notice for the first time that the windows are all boarded up and I wonder if maybe my dad came in and secured the room like this—or if maybe this is a different room altogether and I'm just mixed up.

There's a large box of matches on one of the large, flat, sheet-covered objects—most likely a table of some sort.

I light the first match. The flame ignites blue then yellow, then finally settles in, burning vibrant red and orange.

I pull the sheet away.

Beneath it is a piano—a baby grand. The keys are

brown and yellowed like rotting teeth. A folder of sheet music is open on the piano bench. Some old religious music: "Jesus Make up My Dying Bed."

The match burns down to my fingers then and I curse and blow it out.

Beneath the weathered sheet music is a heavy vinyl record the size of a Frisbee, wrapped in dark-stained wax paper and tied with burlap.

I light another match, holding the record up in one hand and trying to see through the glossy paper. The record seems to carry no markings.

"Jen!" my dad yells sharply.

His voice startles me so I drop the match and have to bat it out with my hand.

"It was open," I say, as if that explains anything.

I turn to face him, but he doesn't seem mad exactly.

"What you got there?" he asks, his smile strained-looking—but still a smile.

"I . . . I don't know," I say. "Some record, I guess."

"Here, let me see."

He takes the record from me and carries it back out into the hallway. As I step out of the room, the cold seems to stay behind me—as though the temperature is somehow relegated to those four walls. The smell, too, seems to remain behind. My dad closes the door and relocks it.

"Don't know how that got open," he says. "Might as well try giving this old record a spin, though, huh? I think I noticed a turntable set up next to the stereo in the living room."

"It doesn't have any label or anything," I say.

He nods.

"Probably homemade. When I was a kid you could record an LP like this at a studio in town for five dollars. Although," he continues, turning the record over a couple times, "this looks much older."

"Older than you?" I say, forcing a smile. "Didn't think that was possible."

He laughs and this strange jocularity makes me fidget uncomfortably.

I keep shifting my weight from one leg to the other.

"Are you feeling better?" he asks me.

I nod.

"Yeah, I guess so," I say.

He smiles, not showing any teeth.

"We've got a lot of work to do," he says. "So . . . uh . . . let's get back to it."

In the kitchen I drink more water from the tap and,

feeling hungry again, and like my stomach can handle a little more food, I decide to take a break from working so I can make myself some eggs.

I get a pan down from one of the cupboards and I'm about to light the burner when I'm startled by the sound of a car coming up the driveway.

My dad must hear it, too, because he calls out to me, "Who is that? Who's coming?"

His footsteps echo down the stairs.

I make my way over to the window and look out to see a rusted pickup truck pulling in next to my dad's Volvo. Beyond the car and the line of trees, I notice a gathering of dark clouds on the horizon—despite the bright sun and perfect blue of the sky overhead. The driver's-side door opens and I'm pretty surprised to see Christy's aunt Rose stepping out.

I turn the faucet on and splash cool water on my face, trying to bring the world back into sharper focus. Rose makes her way up the stairs and I hurry to get to the door before my dad does.

But, of course, I'm too late.

My dad has the door open and is standing with his arms crossed.

"Hello? Can I help you?"

Rose smiles wide. She's wearing a barn coat over jeans and rubber Bean boots. She stares at my father and my father stares back. Strangely, they stay staring like that, back and forth. Rose narrows her eyes at him.

"I know you from somewhere," she says.

My dad forces a smile.

"No, I don't think so. We just moved in here. I'm Anselm Noonan."

"Yes, of course," she says. "I'm sorry. I'm Rose Lynch. I own the Double R Diner in town. I met your wonderful daughter yesterday when she came in to do her homework."

My dad nods, the smile gone now. He stares coldly again.

"I don't mean to pry," Rose tells him. "But I just wanted to check on Jen after what happened last night."

"How'd you know about that?" my dad asks, standing up a little straighter.

I walk up between them.

"Hey, Rose," I say, forcing my own damn smile. "That's nice of you to come."

"Oh, sweetie," she tells me, wrapping her big arms around me and rubbing my back.

I'm not all that comfortable with her touching me,

but I'm too polite to say anything.

"I'm okay," I say, trying to get free of her grip. "I'm really okay."

My dad steps away from the door and asks if Rose wants to come inside. The wind has picked up some, so the leaves are blown out of the dark forest onto the winding driveway. Rose's short gray hair is tied back behind a red bandana.

She holds up a hand to shield her eyes from the wind and dust.

"No . . . no, thank you," she says, staying where she is on the front porch. "I have to get going. I just wanted to make sure you were okay, Jen."

"Yeah," I say. "I'm fine."

"Christy told me she was supposed to come over tonight with some of her friends?"

"Oh yeah," I say. "I forgot about that."

"You don't want to cancel?" Rose asks.

"Jen," my dad says, turning to me. "I don't want you to get distracted. We have a lot of work to do."

"A little company won't hurt her any," Rose says, smiling. "Be a nice thing for Jen after all that happened."

My dad clenches his teeth, but nods.

"Fine," he says. "But just for tonight."

Aunt Rose smiles, then she looks up into the sky, wonderingly.

"Well, I hope you two get outside a little today—take advantage of this fine weather we're having. Gonna be a big storm coming in tomorrow. Weatherman says it could be the biggest storm on record."

She turns her attention to me suddenly and cocks her head to one side.

"But you know that already, don't you?"

I make a face, frowning.

"Me? What do you mean?"

"Oh, nothing," she tells me, smiling. "I just saw you looking at those clouds, too."

"You did?" I ask, confused.

"Come on," my dad says, taking hold of my arm. "You have to get back to work if you want to see your friends tonight."

He nods curtly to Rose.

"Thank you for your concern," he says.

Her turns his back on her and doesn't let go of my arm.

"If you need anything," Rose tells me, "you know where to find me."

My dad pulls me away.

"Let's go," he says.

I look back at Rose.

She smiles at me.

And with my eyes, I try to ask her for help—I try to tell her I'm trapped here with a crazy person. But I can't say it out loud. And so she can't understand. And my dad has me back inside.

He closes the door.

CHAPTER 9

After I finish my chores in the house, my dad wants me to go pull weeds in the garden and, of course, I don't really have a choice. I put on boots and my heavy jacket and a pair of leather gardening gloves and go out into the still-warm afternoon.

The world is coming into focus a little better, the dreamy haze from the pills clearing. I've made little piles of the deep-rooted ragweed and thistles all the way out to the forest and I go grab the rake out of the stone garage and start adding up all the piles into one big pile. It's not difficult work, but already I'm flushed and glossy with sweat. My chest, too, is tender and weirdly bigger-seeming, so I start unfastening my bra.

But then a shiver runs through me and I turn, almost jumping out of my skin as a voice says, "Jen, hey."

It's Colin.

He's half-hidden by the white barren pines.

"Jesus, why are you always lurking behind my house?"

He laughs, keeping his eyes on the ground.

"I'm not lurking."

"You look like you're lurking. Anyway, I told you, my dad's gonna kill me if he sees me talking to you."

"We were supposed to meet up," he says, stepping back into the shadows of the forest. "Don't you remember?"

I nod.

"Oh yeah, right. Sorry."

"Well, do you have time to come talk for a minute?"

I look back at the house, scanning the many windows.

"Yeah, all right," I say. "Just for a minute."

He turns and starts off into the woods and I follow after him.

Leaves colored gold and red and brown cover the forest floor. Birds sing atonally overhead.

"I'm sorry I startled you," he tells me. "But I really wanted to see you."

I breathe out slow.

"It's okay. I'm sorry I forgot. It was a crazy night—and morning."

"Is it true about Alex, then?" he asks.

I stare up at the close together, narrow, spindly, dead-looking trees.

"Jesus, this is a gossipy little town, isn't it?"

He leans his shoulder into me.

"Yeah, it is. We got shit else to do. Anyway, I'm just glad you're all right."

He pauses then before adding, "You are all right, aren't you?"

"Yeah, I'm all right. He's the one who ended up in the hospital."

"The hospital?"

"Uh-huh. I kicked him in the balls and then smashed a picture frame across his face."

Not exactly true, but it seems easier to explain it that way.

"Well, good," he says. "I'm just sorry you had to deal with that."

"Yeah, me, too."

The clouds are moving in quickly from the east and there's a sweet smell like rain in the air.

"It's weird that he would come back here," Colin says.

I look at him curiously.

"What do you mean?"

He scratches at the bridge of his broad nose.

"I mean, this place . . ."

He gestures with both hands.

"Harmony House . . . we used to come sneak in here when we were kids."

"'We'?"

He reddens.

"Yeah, we. We used to be friends. Actually, it was here we had the . . . uh . . . falling-out."

"In the hotel?"

"In the hotel, yeah. Except it wasn't a hotel yet. We broke in through this window over the basement. You been down there yet?"

I shake my head.

"Well, it's creepy as hell. We used to come in on dares and stuff, just to look around or whatever. But, one day, we came in after school and Alex just, like, disappeared. Seriously, I couldn't find him anywhere. I looked and looked, but it was like he'd straight-up fuckin' vanished. And I got, like, lost in all the rooms down there. Then he finally shows up, I mean out of nowhere, and starts like attacking me—hitting me and acting all crazy—like he was really trying to kill me."

"Jesus. What'd you do?"

"What did I do? I kicked his ass, that's what I did. But, ever since then, me 'n Alex have stayed pretty well clear of one another."

Colin looks at me, then, something glinting behind his eyes.

"Tell you what, though," he continues on. "He's scared of me. You won't have to worry about being bothered by him . . . or anybody long as I'm around."

He rubs his hand over his short-cut hair.

I smile.

"I can take care of myself," I tell him.

He laughs. "Yeah, I guess you can."

He pauses then before adding, "I'm just saying."

I turn toward the house again.

"Look," I say. "I'm sorry. I don't think I can hang out right now. I've got chores to finish and some of the girls from town are coming over tonight. Maybe you can come by later."

He seems to think about that.

"How 'bout tomorrow, instead?" he says. "Could you get free in the afternoon?"

I smile.

"Yeah, totally. Like around three? We could go to the beach."

He nods. "Sure, yeah. Only there's a big storm coming in. You heard about that?"

"Yeah. Rose from the diner came by earlier. She told me."

"Rose came by?" he says. "That's good. I'm glad she's checking up on you."

"Oh yeah," I say, scratching at the back of my neck. "She seems a little weird to me."

He laughs.

"Well, she's a medium. So, yeah, she's weird."

"A medium?" I ask, frowning. "You mean she talks to dead people?"

He shrugs.

"She thinks she does. Anyway, she's good at reading people. She picks up on things. They call it cold reading."

"Does she charge people for these readings?"

"No. No. It's not like that. But I trust her. If she told

me something, I'd believe it."

I narrow my eyes at him.

"Something like what?"

He laughs more.

"I don't know. Anything."

I think about that.

"She did tell me one thing," I say, chewing on my lower lip again. "She told me I already knew the storm was coming. And when I asked her how I knew, she said she'd seen me looking at the clouds. Only I hadn't looked at the clouds. At least, not in front of her."

"See?" he says, smiling. "I told you, she just knows things."

"Yeah," I say. "But the way she told it to me . . . I don't know. There was something . . ."

I laugh then and shake my head.

"Never mind. I don't know what I'm talking about."

He laughs with me.

"It's okay. Like I said, I'm just glad she's looking out for you."

He puts a hand on my shoulder, but gently, and adds, "I am, too, you know? I'm looking out for you."

I nod.

I don't pull away.

"Thank you," I say. "That actually means a lot to me."

I smile as best I can.

And he smiles back at me.

I can't help but blush.

"I should go," I tell him.

"Yeah, okay."

"But I'll try to get free tomorrow," I say.

He smiles.

"Good."

"Thank you," I say again.

He kisses me quickly on the cheek.

"I'll see you tomorrow," he tells me.

I blush more.

I turn, starting back toward the house.

My heart is racing and I feel a dropping out in my stomach.

The last thing I need, I tell myself, is to get involved with a boy here in Beach Haven. I've got enough fucking trouble.

I think about what he said—about Rose being some kind of medium. My mom was always into stuff like that. I guess spiritualists and fortune-tellers and astrologers and palm readers and numerologists—and preachers—and cult leaders make it their business to prey on the weak and desperate. And my mom certainly was that. She was about the most weak and desperate person I ever met.

She used to read books about the moon phases and what planets were in retrograde and all that bullshit. She tried meditation workshops and weird seminars with yogis and self-help gurus and rebirthing therapies and est training and Synanon and, yes, even Christian/Catholic/Evangelical/whatever religion like my dad. She tried everything—except stopping drinking. And she never stuck with any one thing for long—except, again, for the drinking.

Last year she even tried AA. But then, too, she never stopped drinking.

She'd gotten a DUI was all, and the judge ordered her to a mandatory ninety in ninety. She had a slip of paper she had to get signed. And she used to make me drive her to the meetings.

I remember one time, right at the end, when I drove her to the public park in Johnstown where they had baseball diamonds and a playground and a few ratty, cracked concrete tennis courts. I parked and my mom did a lot of breathing and sighing and saying, "Goddammit! Let's get this over with."

"Come on, it's not so bad," I said, trying to be encouraging.

I rolled up the window and opened the door and the key ding-ding-dinged in the ignition.

"It's ridiculous," she said. "I mean, how stupid do they think I am?"

She snatched the keys out and put them in her pocket and told me to hurry. I didn't argue with her, grabbing a book I'd brought with me out of the backseat—*Wuthering Heights*. I climbed out into the fading heat of the early summer day-turning-night.

"They say it's a disease," she told me, baring her teeth—whispering like someone might hear. "But then they say the only way to recover is to pray."

I looked up at her through the dark bangs over my eyes.

"If I had cancer," she said, "would they tell me to pray to recover from that? Jesus Christ. Is it a disease, or isn't it? They need to make up their minds. They sound just like your father."

"But it can help you," I said, watching as other people began parking their cars and gathering in front of the rec center, smoking cigarettes and talking loudly—laughing, hugging each other, slapping each other on the back, shaking hands. "It's worth a try, anyway."

My mom seemed to watch them, too.

She took hold of my hand and pulled me closer.

She crouched down, speaking close in my ear.

"It works for them," she said, gesturing toward the growing crowd. "It's made them better. But it will never work for me."

I remember my stomach aching then. I remember being chilled. I wanted to go home and turn the TV on and the volume up like when I was a little kid.

"But . . . why?" I asked, staring down at a piece of gum, smashed and blackened in the sidewalk.

She was silent for a moment. I could hear the talking all around us like the drone of insects swarming. There was the smell of mouthwash and toothpaste masking something acrid and bitter on my mom's breath.

"I'm not like them," she said. "I'm different."

"But, Mom—"

She didn't let me finish.

"Nothing can help me," she said.

And when I looked at her again, there were tears in her eyes.

"Please," I said. "You've got to give it a chance."

"I've looked for answers my whole life," she said,

facing me—not looking away. "And the only answer I ever found is that there is no answer. I'm sorry, Jen. But that's the truth. Maybe it'll be different for you. Maybe you'll find something; I never did."

"Please, Mom," I said again. "Please."

"It doesn't matter," she said. "It makes no difference at all."

She let go of my hand and walked off into the meeting. I saw her get coffee for herself in a Styrofoam cup and take a seat at the back.

I went over to the playground and sat on a bench and read my book.

My mom was dead two months later.

Maybe she found the answer she was looking for in death, but I don't believe that.

All I know is that if there are answers out there, they don't come from any bullshit self-help groups or religious zealots—or goddamn mediums. If that's what Rose calls herself, then I sure as hell don't want anything to do with her. She may seem like a harmless old lady, but I've seen just how much harm those claiming to have "answers" can do to the weak and desperate people of this world. My mom needed real help, real solutions, not a bunch of party tricks.

There's a heat rising in me now.

I clench my fists.

I want to tear everything down around me.

I want to scream and rage.

The sun is starting to set over the distant hills. The black clouds gather. The wind blows steadily.

Near the clearing, by a little stream, I trip over something hard and curse and bend down to take hold of my throbbing ankle—the pain there jumping up my leg.

With my gloved hands I dig through the rank, stinking leaves to see what the hell it was I tripped over. Insects scatter in all directions as I reveal their hiding places and inadvertently dig them up. A long centipede flips on its back, legs fanning like an underwater creature. I give a little shriek and fling it away from me as far as I can.

But soon the dirt and leaves and twigs and pine needles and insects and loose rocks are cleared away. My breath catches. My lungs strain tight. What I see on the ground beside me is a headstone, cracked and oddly small—moss-covered, with the words mostly worn away. In fact, I can't make out the name—only the date: November 11, 1919. That is all. Nothing else.

Absently I begin digging through surrounding piles of leaves.

My hand lands on another small stone—

Then there is another stone—and then another. Frantically I throw the leaves away—revealing a cemetery of tiny graves. Most of them, like the first, have only one date. But a few have two—always close together. July 7, 1914–July 9, 1914. April 23, 1926–April 24, 1926. December 22, 1930–January 1, 1931.

Dead babies.

A field of them. Unnamed, mostly.

Only the initials *CSM*.

Chilled, I stand, brushing the dirt off my knees.

I leave the tiny graves uncovered.

I step out into the clearing and pick up the rake and start gathering up the piles of dead weeds, trying not to think of anything—trying my best to block it all out.

I work until the sun has set.

Then I go back inside, where music plays from a vintage-looking record player in the living room by a fire my dad has built up. He sits staring at the flames—orange and red and pale yellow lapping at the blackened bricks. The light from the fire reflects like shadow puppets across my dad's weathered face and neck and arms. Tearstains are all down his cheeks—his bloodshot eyes are swollen.

And then I hear the woman's voice coming through the built-in speakers.

*"I . . . fall . . . to pieces . . . each time someone speaks . . .
your name."*

"Is this that record?" I ask, still standing in the doorway.

But my dad doesn't answer.

He stares straight ahead.

I walk up quietly behind him and sit on the cracked
leather sofa.

The music is beautiful—haunting—and the singer's
voice sounds so familiar somehow—like my mother's
voice, I think.

Except my mother is dead.

And the woman singing isn't her.

"Dad," I say again.

But he won't even look at me.

More than anything, now, I'm seized with this
panic, like I have to get out of this room—away from
this music.

I cover my ears with my hands and begin to run.

The voice like my mother's plays over and over in
my mind.

I run up the stairs back to my room.

I close the door behind me, gasping for breath.

"What the hell was that?" I say out loud.

I try to think, was my mom ever a singer?

But, obviously, she was not.

The only logical explanation is that I'm going fucking crazy here.

I take another one of the pink oblong pills from the bag in my jacket lining and dry-swallow it and then, well, fuck it, right? I take another.

I go lie perpendicularly across the bed, staring up at the cracked and stained pink-painted ceiling. The girls from town will be coming soon. I need to shower and change. But my body feels so heavy. I can't help but close my eyes. And, with my eyes closed, I can't help but sleep—and, in sleep, to dream. And in my dream, to be back in my bed upstairs in the noxious pink room—the blankets thick and smelling of lavender. It is the middle of the night and the stars outside the window shine brilliantly. Reaching over to turn on the light next to my bed I realize that, for some reason, the lamp has disappeared. In its place is an old-fashioned oil-burning lantern and a box of matches. My nightgown, too, is old-fashioned—white—frilled around the collar.

There's a noise like scratching at the glass and as I roll onto my side I see the window start to open.

Instantly my heart pounds loud and painful in my chest and I feel sick and icy and drenched with sweat.

A figure crawls in through the open window.

It is Alex, I think, just like before.

But then the figure is on top of me and he's bigger than Alex—thick, sweating. He smells of cut grass and hay and something sour. He gets hold of my wrist and I cry out, but then his hand closes on my mouth and my voice is muffled and I struggle for breath. His body pins me down. Tears run hot down my cheeks.

The body moves on top of me.

And only then do I see his face.

It emerges from out of the shadows.

It is the father's face. The father from the family portraits at Harmony House.

Only now his eyes bulge—red-veined, terrible.

His hand moves.

And, finally, I scream.

The scream wakes me.

I'm on the bed, but not under the covers, and the sun is just starting to set over the vascular-hued sky.

Looking over at the clock on the bedside table, I see it's nearly five thirty.

I force myself up and off the bed.

I go down the hall to the bathroom and turn the shower on hot.

I let the water burn my skin red.

I stand beneath the spray coming down.

The pain is like holding my hand over the flame of a gas stove.

But I take it, and take it, and take it.

Until I can't take it anymore.

And I turn the cold water on.

And crouch down on the heels of my feet.

And hug my knees to my chest.

And wait to feel clean.

CHAPTER 10

My dad went up to bed pretty early, thankfully, so I didn't have to be *too* totally embarrassed by him in front of Christy and Candace and Mercedes. He did make me promise, before the girls got here, to try and spread the word of God and salvation to them. He gave me a big, long, crazy lecture about how I need to lead the flock and pass on the holy word to the poor sinners of the world and blah, blah, blah. I have no idea why he's acting so totally insane these days. He even started proselytizing to the girls a little bit. Both Candace and

Mercedes had guys they wanted to invite over, but after spending a little time with my dad, and I guess hearing about everything that happened last night, they called their respective boy toys and held them off.

So now the three girls and I have made up a big bed on the floor in the back sitting room, where there's a TV and VCR. We have a fire going and we're eating microwave popcorn and drinking hot chocolate.

The girls, surprisingly to me, had not seen *The Silence of the Lambs*, so we've started with that, and they all seem pretty freaked out. That storm really must be coming, too, because it's raining hard outside and the wind is blowing the rain against the downstairs windows, making a rat-a-tat-tat sound over and over and over again.

On the television Anthony Hopkins has just ripped the prison guard's face off with his teeth and the girls all scream and I laugh at them, but just 'cause they're cute and obviously not into weird, dark shit like I am. There's a pain in my stomach, cutting in, though, not related to the movie, that makes me feel dizzy and nauseous and I have to get up from where we're sitting and go off down the hall to find the bathroom.

"Where are you going?" Candace asks me.

And Mercedes almost cries, "You can't leave us here."

I try to smile and say, "I'm sorry. I'll be right back."

And I go out of the room quickly, feeling the nausea rising up in my throat.

On my way to the bathroom, fighting the urge to be sick all over the floor, I hear an unfamiliar sound drifting in from the other room—the sound of a strange, rhythmic chanting—over and over—high-pitched— with something deeper and guttural underneath. I am chilled, so the nausea is momentarily forgotten.

The sudden cold makes my fingers numb.

That smell of pungent mold and mildew is almost palpable.

I pass through the foyer and the dining room and the reading library and the study, and the chanting and screaming and shrieking gets louder and louder. The house seems to swell and exhale around me—the walls and ceiling pushing in and drawing back. I wonder how the girls haven't heard anything from the other room yet.

A fire is burning again in the living room fireplace— immense, bright, casting shadows like leaves falling from the trees outside. The record player is rotating rhythmically and it looks like that record I found earlier, the sound worse than any horror I could ever imagine—worse, even, than that scream the man screamed realizing he'd just taken another man's life with his car. The sound makes me want to tear my skin off and gouge out my eyes.

I look over at the huddled figure by the fire.

I see my father standing, hunched and rocking back and forth, sweat covering his face—his hair dripping with it—his pale skin almost translucent in the firelight.

"Dad!" I shout, startling myself.

My dad turns to stare at me, though his eyes are milky and vacant. He teeters and stands slack-jawed. Slowly he begins stepping toward me.

Unable to take it one more fucking second, I run and switch the player off.

I look up from the turntable just in time to see my dad walking dazedly out of the room, muttering to himself, babbling. I call out again, but he keeps walking. I hear him stumbling from room to room.

I turn the heavy vinyl over in my hand, then, before I can stop myself, throw it in the fire.

A cold wind tunnels through the rooms as I hear the heavy front door, swollen in its frame, pushed open—followed by more footsteps down the front stairs and out into the night. The rain smells sweet through the open door and the wind carries fallen leaves into the front room.

My stomach lurches, and I rush back inside to the downstairs bathroom—cramped and narrow—just managing to turn the faucet on before vomiting up what feels like the entire contents of my stomach. I've been throwing up so much at this point, it feels like . . . what's that expression? Old hat? But, no, that's not true. It sucks as much as always. I choke and spit and flush the vomit down and then lie on the cool tile.

Soon there is a knocking at the door.

"Jen, are you okay?"

It's Christy's voice.

Then I hear Candace ask, "Was it the movie?"

And Mercedes says, "Can we get you anything."

It makes me feel kind of good, honestly, that all three of them came to check on me. Though maybe it's just that none of them wanted to be left alone in this supposedly haunted fucking house. Either way I appreciate it.

"I'm all right," I call out. "I've just been sick recently."

"Maybe she's pregnant," I hear Candace say.

"Yeah, right," says Mercedes.

The thought chills me. But I shake my head and try to forget it. I get up off the bathroom floor and go open the door.

"Sorry," I say, sweating a little. "I don't know what's wrong with me."

"We were just worried about you," Christy says.

I turn back to the sink and splash some water on my face and drink from the faucet before turning it off.

"You want to go get some air?" Mercedes asks. "I think it stopped raining."

"I'd kill for a cigarette," I say.

"I have a pack of Lucky Strikes," says Mercedes.

"Lucky Strikes," I say. "Those are like old-man cigarettes."

"I stole 'em from my grandfather," Mercedes says.

I laugh.

"All right, but if we go outside, my dad'll hear us. He's a total creeper. Let's go down in the basement. It'll be warmer anyway."

"The basement!" Christy says, kind of horrified-sounding. "Really?"

"Why? Are you scared?" Mercedes asks her, smiling.

"No . . . yeah . . . kind of."

"Come on," says Candace. "It'll be all right."

"Okay," I say. "This way."

I lead them down the uneven, splintered wooden stairs, turning on the bare overhead lightbulb and making my way over to a small rectangular window. Piled everywhere are cardboard boxes and more furniture covered in white linens and stacks of shelving with more boxes. The smell of mildew is overpowering. A complicated maze of different pipes and wires runs the length of the ceiling—the insulation is exposed and even falling down in places. The concrete floor is stained and cracked and there's about an inch of brackish water pooled in one corner.

"Your dad may be a creeper," Mercedes says, "but it's pretty damn creepy down here, too."

"It's not any warmer, either," says Christy.

She's right, of course. The cold is penetrating. And the mildew smell is mixed with that same rotting-animal smell.

I go quickly to the window and open it.

"Here," say Mercedes, handing me a cigarette.

She takes one herself and so does Candace. Only Christy declines.

We light the cigarettes with an orange lighter Mercedes has in her purse.

I inhale and exhale.

"What'd you guys think of the movie so far?"

"Scary," says Christy.

"Really scary," says Candace. "I remember my dad telling me after he and my mom saw it in the theaters he actually looked in the backseat of the car to make sure no one was hiding there before they drove home."

I laugh.

"So are your parents still together, then?" I ask.

"Yeah," she says.

"So are mine," says Mercedes.

"So are mine," says Christy.

"Well, aren't we all anomalies? I mean, my mom's dead," I say, "but my parents never got divorced."

We are all silent for a minute.

"Sometimes I wish mine would get divorced," says Christy.

I turn to her, surprised.

"The way they fight," she continues, "I think they'd be better off."

"Mine would've been, too," I say. "Definitely."

"How did your mom die?" Mercedes asks, tentatively—and then adds, "You don't have to tell us."

The cold seems to fill the room even more biting and I shiver.

"No, it's okay," I say. "She . . . uh . . . she was an alcoholic. She asphyxiated on . . . uh . . . her own . . . you know . . . throw-up."

"Like Jimi Hendrix," Mercedes says.

Candace comes over and puts her hand on my shoulder.

"I'm sorry that happened to you," she says.

"Yeah, it sucks," I tell them.

"My parents are still together," Mercedes says. "But . . . uhmm . . . if you wanna know the truth . . . my mom's had a lot of . . . uh . . . substance-abuse issues, too. She's been to rehab a whole bunch of times. And my dad travels all the time for work. So it's mostly my grandparents who raised me."

"Damn," says Candace. "My family's so normal, I feel almost bad."

"Don't," I tell her. "You're lucky."

I stub my cigarette out and the other girls do, too, and I gather the three butts up and hide them under one of the piles of boxes.

"I wish we had something to drink," says Mercedes.

"I've got Cokes up in the fridge," I tell her.

She laughs.

"No, I mean . . . something to *drink*, drink."

"Oh," I tell her, laughing, too. "Well, I might be able

to steal some from my dad."

"I'm down with that," says Christy.

But then a gust of wind slams the window shut and we all jump and the light overhead flares bright and then pops loudly, leaving us immersed in pure, perfect blackness. Candace is standing close to me and I can hear her quick shallow breathing and I reach out and take her hand. She squeezes tight and I hold on.

"Don't worry," I say, trying to keep my voice steady. "This happened last night, too. It's just the circuit breaker."

The sound of Candace's breathing grows louder and more strained, like she's having an asthma attack.

"Candace. Are you okay?" I ask.

"Well, I can't see," she says.

But her voice comes from across the room. She's not next to me at all.

My legs start to shake. I feel the hand grip me tighter.

"C-Christy?" I call out.

The hand holding mine is crushing me now.

"Ow, let go," I yell.

And then I hear Christy.

She's not next to me, either.

"Who are you talking to?" she says.

I feel the hand release.

My heart beats so I feel dizzy, and I reach out in all directions, but no one is there.

"This isn't funny," I say.

"What?" asks Candace.

I can't slow my breathing down. I feel like I might pass out from the panic making me tremble all over. And then that same hand is pushing me now—pushing me harder and harder.

"Please," I say, my voice cracking. "Please. Stop it!"

"Jen, stop messing around," Mercedes says.

But I'm being pushed by this hand up against the wall—face-first into the rough concrete.

"STOP IT!" I yell as loud as I can.

And then another pop sounds and just as suddenly as the light switched off, it comes flaring back on. We all seem to gasp collectively and blink our eyes. The wall in front of me slowly begins to take shape. A warm trickle of blood runs down from my forehead where I was pressed up against the concrete.

"What the hell was that?" Mercedes yells at me. "Was that some kind of joke?"

I turn to face her, tears welling in my eyes—spilling over, mixing with the blood.

"Jesus Christ," she says, running over to me.

And then Candace screams.

"You guys! You guys!"

"What?" I ask, wiping my face with the back of my hand.

"Christy's gone."

Mercedes and I both turn to look.

Candace is right.

Christy isn't there.

"Christy!" I call out.

The other girls begin looking around for her.

"Did you see her leave?" I ask stupidly.

Mercedes shakes her head. "It was dark."

Candace wraps her arms around herself and shivers.

"Where could she have gone?" she asks.

"I didn't hear anything," Mercedes says. "Did you?"

"No," I say.

I can see that both girls are shaking now, the way I am.

"What the fuck *was* that?" Mercedes says.

"I just got scared," I say, not wanting to tell either one of them the truth. "I must've gotten turned around and I ran into the wall."

"Yeah, but where the hell is Christy?" Candace asks.

The sound of the wind coming in through the vents above us is high-pitched, like an animal whimpering.

"She must've run back upstairs," I say.

"I didn't hear her," Mercedes says.

"No," I say. "But she must've."

Candace moves toward the stairs.

"Let's get out of here," she says.

Mercedes nods and we all start up toward the main floor together, the steps creaking beneath our weight.

"No offense, Jen, but this house seriously sucks," Mercedes says.

"Yeah, no shit," I say.

We reach the first-floor hallway and I shut off the basement light and close the door firmly behind me.

"Christy!" I call out, looking in both directions.

She doesn't answer, though, and I don't see her anywhere.

"Jesus Christ," says Mercedes. "This is crazy."

I feel my face flush red.

"I'm sorry," I say. "I didn't mean for everything to get so . . . weird like this."

Candace puts a hand on my shoulder and I see her exchange a glance with Mercedes.

"It's not your fault," she says.

"Yeah," says Mercedes. "And I'm sure Christy just went back to the TV room or something."

"Of course," I say. "You're right."

We go together, walking close, back to the TV room, calling out for Christy all the while. The lights along the hall seem dimmer than I remember them, as though the house isn't getting enough electricity from the lines outside. We pass through several rooms, badly lit and dark-colored—the walls brown—with dust on every surface, though I cleaned this morning. When we finally come to the room where we set up our sleeping things, the TV is playing a grainy static so the blacks and whites flash like a strobe across the room.

"Dammit," says Candace, once she realizes Christy isn't here. "Where the hell could she have gone?"

I breathe out, shaking my head.

"Maybe the kitchen?" I say.

Mercedes rubs at the back of her neck with her small hands.

"This just doesn't make any sense," she says.

I repeat that I'm sorry.

We go now to the kitchen.

"Christy!" I yell as we walk. "Christy!"

I yell it 'til my voice is hoarse and I feel like I want to cry.

But she's not in the kitchen, either.

"Could she have gone outside?"

I look out the window.

"Her car's still there," I say.

I can see it parked in the gravel, surrounded by the coming mist like a spiderweb. The rain has stopped and the sky is clear. The moon, half-full, casts a silvery light across the driveway.

"Maybe she went to your room," Candace says.

Mercedes and I both nod together.

"Yeah, maybe."

We start back through the front entranceway and climb the stairs, yelling Christy's name over and over and over.

When we reach the top floor, I lead the girls into my disgustingly pink, girly room.

Pieces of paper are spread out all across the floor. They are pages from a book—from that prayer book. It lies open on my bed, the pages all torn out of it.

Nausea makes me dizzy so I have to shut my eyes.

"What happened here?" Candace asks.

I shake my head slowly.

"I . . . I don't know. It wasn't like this when I left it."

I open my eyes to see Mercedes is holding one of the pages in her hand—that same Prayer of Saint Francis.

Only now even more of the words have been blacked out.

~~Lord, make me an instrument of Your~~
~~peace~~
~~Where there is~~ hatred, ~~let me sow love~~
~~Where there is~~ injury, ~~pardon~~
~~Where there is discord, harmony~~
~~Where there is error, truth~~
~~Where there is doubt, faith~~
~~Where there is~~ despair, ~~hope~~
~~Where there is~~ darkness, ~~light~~
~~And where there is sadness, joy.~~
~~O Divine Master, grant that I may not~~
~~so much seek~~
~~To be consoled as to console~~
~~To be understood as to understand~~
~~To be loved as to love.~~
~~For it is in giving that we receive~~
~~It is in pardoning that we are pardoned~~
~~And it is in~~ dying ~~that we are born to~~
eternal ~~life.~~

Hatred, injury, despair, darkness, dying, eternal.
"Did you do this?" Mercedes asks.

"No," I say. "No, I swear."

I open my hand and let the page flutter gently to the floor.

"I am officially fucking freaked out," Candace says.

I nod.

"Me, too."

"Where the hell is Christy?" Mercedes asks.

"We have to find her now," I say, though I'm not totally sure why.

And so we start down the stairs again, still calling her name. We reach the second floor and start toward my dad's room.

We walk pressed close together. The lights flare with surges of electricity. A big dresser is pressed up against one of the dark-colored walls. The shadow of the dresser reaches out across the hallway. I take a step and then another step.

A figure emerges from the shadow and I jump a fucking mile. Candace screams and Mercedes grabs my arm tight.

It's Christy.

She's standing in the middle of the hall, just a few feet from my dad's room. Her head is down and her arms hang by her sides. Her face is colorless and her lips slightly blue around the edges like she isn't breathing.

"Christy!" Mercedes says, running toward her. "Oh, thank God!"

She hugs Christy to her, but Christy's body remains limp. She teeters slightly. Her eyes are all black and distant. She stares, but with unfocused eyes.

"Where were you?" Candace asks. "We were so worried."

Christy then looks up at her, but her eyes don't seem to fix on any one point.

"I have to go," Christy says—so weakly it's almost inaudible.

"What?" Mercedes shouts at her. "We were worried. Where the hell were you?"

Christy goes on staring straight past us. Her slack body begins to move as though gliding to the stairs.

"I'm sorry," she says. "I have to go."

"Wait!" I say.

I grab her by the arm, but her skin is so cold and lifeless-feeling, I let go and back away from her.

She keeps on to the edge of the banister.

"What happened?" Mercedes asks. "Talk to us."

Christy doesn't answer.

She grabs hold of the banister with both hands.

"What are you doing?" Candace asks.

Christy's expression never changes.

"I have to go," she says.

And then in one quick movement, she lifts herself up on the railing and jumps.

"Jesus, no!" I yell.

But I'm too late.

Her body free-falls for several seconds.

And then there is a loud crash below.

And then no sound at all.

CHAPTER 11

The lights flash red, blue, red, and then blue again—reflecting off the windows and the badge of the officer in front of me.

I wrap my arms tightly around my chest and shiver against the clear, cold night. The sweet smell of rain is in the air still. The moon shines like a pearl in the starless sky.

"Why don't you go on in and get a jacket?" Sheriff Jarrett says, noticing me shivering. "Don't want you catching cold out here."

I tell him I'm all right.

He shakes his head.

"Been a rough couple days for you. Don't want you getting sick on top of that."

Again, I tell him I'm all right.

I watch as the ambulance doors slam shut and the siren sounds and it tears on up the driveway to the road. I can see Mercedes and Candace in the back of the sheriff's police car. Candace is crying and shaking all over. Mercedes is still and quiet.

Sheriff Jarrett follows my gaze. "EMT says her ribs are fractured and her legs and wrists are broken, but she'll recover."

I shake my head.

"God, I feel terrible."

He puts a large hand on my shoulder.

"Don't worry," he tells me. "It's not your fault."

And then he laughs.

"You're just unlucky, I guess."

I force a smile.

"I guess I am."

He drops his head.

"Anyway, she'll be all right. That's what's important."

I nod.

"Yeah. I just can't figure out why she would've jumped like that."

Sheriff Jarrett shrugs.

"Fear does strange things to people."

He pauses a second, then gestures with his head. "It does strange things to people in that house."

"So I gathered," I tell him.

He frowns then, looking hard at me. He reaches a hand out and gingerly touches my collarbone.

"What happened here?" he asks.

I try to see what he's pointing at.

"What do you mean?"

"Those bruises," he says. "Pretty nasty."

"Oh God, yeah," I tell him, reddening. "I forgot about those. I'm not sure where they came from."

He glances back at the house, then at his idling cruiser, then back at me. He speaks in a hoarse whisper.

"If there's anything you want to tell me," he says, "I can protect you. I can make sure you're safe."

I almost laugh out loud at that, but I hold it together. I mean, what? Is he going to protect me from the rantings of my father? Or whatever the hell that was in the basement? Or the voices I've been hearing? Or the craziness in my own mind?

Maybe he has a couple of extra straitjackets he can lend me. One for me and one for my dad.

"No," I say, not holding his gaze. "No, I'm okay. Anyway, it's the truth. I don't know how I got these."

His shoulders rise and fall with an intake of breath.

"Okay, well, you know where to find me. I'll try 'n come by to check in. There's a big storm supposed to be hittin' us tomorrow night. You tell your dad to make sure you got plenty of provisions . . . just in case."

The door to the house bangs open then, and my dad comes out holding what I recognize as Christy's handbag. My stomach tightens a little at the sight of him.

He'd been in the kitchen when I'd come screaming for help, screaming that Christy had jumped. Just sitting at the table, like nothing had even happened.

"Found this in the TV room," he says. "Must belong to one of the girls."

"It's Christy's," I say.

The sheriff takes the purse from my dad and thanks him.

"I'll make sure the family gets it."

And then he adds, "Staffordshire Township Hospital's not too far out of town. I were you, I might think about payin' her a little visit tomorrow. I'm sure the family would appreciate that."

My dad nods stiffly.

"Yes, of course."

"But as I told your daughter here," the sheriff says, "big storm's due to hit us around midnight tomorrow. You'll wanna be sure to have plenty of fresh water, flashlights, batteries, and some canned goods in case the road to town gets blocked."

"Jesus . . . ," I start to say, but change it in my mouth to something like "Jesajeez."

I swallow uncomfortably before continuing, "Is it really going to be that bad?"

For the second time, the sheriff shrugs.

"That's what they're sayin'."

My dad nods, smiling.

"We'll be sure to stock up on a few things."

"All right, then," the sheriff says. "Better get these girls home."

He turns to look directly at my dad now—the two of them about equal height, so their eyes stare back and forth.

"You take care of this daughter of yours, you hear? She's a good girl."

My dad takes a step back.

"Yes, of course," he says. "Thank you for your concern."

He extends his hand awkwardly out in front of him.

"We'll be praying for you, Sheriff. And we'll be praying for that poor young girl, too."

The sheriff shakes my dad's hand, but there is a flicker of recognition in his eyes now—like he can see, all at once, that something isn't quite right with this man standing in front of him. The sheriff keeps on smiling, though, and he wishes us both a good night, saying, again, that he'll come by to check on us—and the house—tomorrow.

He walks down the steps and across the gravel driveway.

He gets in his car.

Mercedes and Candace are in the backseat, both of them quiet now and still. As the car pulls away, they don't turn to look at me. I watch them go. And I know that they will never come back. A thought comes to me then, clear as my own voice speaking out loud—I will never see them again. And while there's no reason why that should be the case, somehow I think it must be true.

"Come on," my dad says. "Let's go inside. I want us to pray together for your friend. God will heal her. If she is worthy, he will relieve her suffering."

I dig my nails into my palms again—the pain making it so I don't spit in my dad's face. He puts a hand heavily on my shoulder.

"We'll ask God to forgive her," he says.

He releases me then and walks back toward the open door.

The outside spotlight attracts mosquitos and gray, dusty moths and crickets the size of clothespins. It glints off the ring on my dad's left hand. It's the ring I found. The gold band with the coiling snakes around a red center stone.

I start to say something, to ask him why he's wearing it.

But no sound comes out.

My voice is as silent and useless as when you try to cry out in a dream.

"Hurry up now," my dad says, turning back to look at me with his eyes hollowed out above dark circles.

I follow him into the house and he closes and locks the door behind me.

"We'll pray for forgiveness for ourselves, too," he says. "We need to be forgiven."

In the light of the hall his skin is so pale I can see all

the blue-green veins rising beneath the surface.

"Dad?" I say, finding my voice again.

He turns to look at me.

I feel my legs start to tremble.

"Are you sure you're all right?" I ask.

His smile is what it must look like if a corpse were to smile. There's no life in it. His lips are upturned and parted. He shows his straight white teeth.

"Before. You were listening to that record," I say. "You walked off into the woods in the middle of the night."

"What record?" he asks. "What are you talking about? Were you drinking? Is that what's going on?"

"I'm trying to tell you," I say, holding myself back from reaching out and strangling him. "You were listening to that record—the one we found. And then you started walking out of the house, talking to yourself— like you couldn't even hear me."

My dad shakes his head.

"You must be tired," he says. "Maybe you dreamed it."

"Dad!" I say.

He stares blankly into a dark corner of the room.

Again, I am chilled.

"Why don't you get some sleep," he finally says. "I'll

go pray for your friend. I'll take care of it. You go up to bed."

"But Dad," I say.

He holds a hand up to me.

"You're just overtired," he says. "That must be it. Now go to bed."

"But . . ."

"Go on," he tells me.

His expression doesn't change. His words are flat and inflectionless. He stands teetering.

I decide not to argue with him.

I do what he says.

I go up to bed.

And, surprisingly, maybe, I do fall asleep.

In the unconsciousness of a fitful sleep, I dream. And in the dream the house becomes the house as it was before. A young girl cries—screams—tears at her hair and skin. Her white dressing gown is soaked with dark, almost black blood. The older nun is there holding an infant in her arms. The infant is dead, bloated, its face blue, its lips purple. The girl cries louder. She screams, "Why? Why?"

The older nun speaks. Her voice is cruel, hoarse, ugly. She mimics the girl, saying, "Why? You know why. Because you are a sinner. This is what you deserve. God is punishing you. He will go on punishing you. You are evil. You are full of the devil. You are going straight to hell."

And then the little boy approaches—the boy with the dark hair. He runs down the hall toward the nun. His fists are clenched and he screams now, "Stop it! Stop it!" He crashes headlong into the older nun—still screaming and hitting her.

The nun's eyes flash as she looks down at the boy, her face flushed red. Cradling the dead infant in one arm, she reaches out fast as a snake and strikes the boy hard across the face. He falls back and tears stream down his cheeks. The nun gnashes her teeth and hits him again, even harder.

The boy cowers on the floor. Then the nun takes the dead child and shows it off to the boy, holding it out just in front of his face.

"This is what happens," she says. "This is what happens to sinners like you."

The boy cries hysterically, trying to close his eyes, but the nun pries them open.

From behind them the young nun—the pretty one—Sister Margaret—with a voice like my mother's—comes up and grabs hold now of the older nun's arm.

"That's enough, Sister Angelica," she says.

The older nun turns on her.

"What did you say to me?" she asks. "You dare talk back to your superiors?"

Sister Margaret shrinks back, but still she tells her, "Leave the boy alone. He's too young to understand."

The older nun, Sister Angelica, shows her gray, crooked teeth. Then she slaps Sister Margaret across the face now, too.

"Your relationship with this boy isn't natural," Sister Angelica tells her, spitting the words out.

The boy springs up off the floor and runs to Sister Margaret's defense.

"Don't touch her," the boy shouts. "Keep your hands off her."

Sister Angelica grabs the boy around the throat and gnashes those same gray teeth. "Evil child, you will rot in hell!"

"Stop it," Sister Margaret says. Her voice is very weak.

And then the monsignor walks heavily up the wooden hallway. They are on the third floor of the house. His footsteps echo up to the rooftops and then down again. He has a wide, porcine face with a small, upturned nose. His blond hair is slicked back above his veined, massive forehead. His hands are small but he has long, manicured fingernails. And on the finger of his left hand, he wears a ring—the gold ring with coiled serpents around a red stone.

Silently, the monsignor grabs the boy from the older nun and flings him brutally into the wall. The boy's head snaps back and cracks loudly. The monsignor turns to Sister Margaret.

"Come with me," he says, hissing like a coiled serpent.

Sister Margaret shudders visibly, her cheek red and swelling from Sister Angelica's slap. She bows her head and walks slowly behind the monsignor. The boy runs after them, pleading, "No, no!"

"Silence," the monsignor says to him. And he is silent.

The monsignor opens the door to a small room off the main hall. Inside, crucifixes adorn the walls—hundreds of them—covering the walls completely. There is a standing wardrobe built of dark wood and inlaid with gold crosses. The young sister enters. The monsignor closes the door behind them. The boy wails and cries.

From within he hears the lashing of the whip and the pitiful whimpering of Sister Margaret.

"Mea culpa," she whispers. "Mea culpa."

The sound of the whip is like a bone breaking.

The boy drops to his knees.

And the whip sounds again.

And again.

And again.

CHAPTER 12

In the morning I am sick again. I vomit in the upstairs bathroom and lie curled on the cold tile floor waiting for the nausea and dizziness to pass. There are more purplish-yellow bruises up and down my arms and my muscles ache. Looking up through the bathroom window, I see the sky has turned gray with rain clouds and a strong wind makes the branches of the trees thrash wildly in all directions.

I think back on everything that happened yesterday. I shiver and my head spins and then I am sick again.

I can't understand what the hell is wrong with me. I remember then something Mercedes said last night before all the craziness with Christy. She said maybe I was pregnant.

I know it was a joke—but maybe it's true.

I mean, it's definitely not impossible.

I put my hands on my stomach, trying to feel . . . what? If there's a baby in there? The thought makes me want to get sick all over again. I know I should be worrying about Christy breaking both her goddamn legs. And I *am* worried about her. But if I'm pregnant—Jesus Christ. I need to find out as soon as possible.

There's a pain in my head like the veins swelling so I can feel my pulse beating like a screw being rhythmically turned and tightened.

Staggering back to my room, I take two of the off-white-colored pills from the bag in my jacket lining and then lie back in bed with my eyes closed waiting to be taken away from whatever this is.

I'm not sure how long I lie there like that before the pills start to make the sickness and everything else disappear. I breathe in and out. Then there is a knock on my door and my dad walks in without waiting for me to answer.

"What are you doing still in bed?" he barks at me.

I sit up a little unsteadily—holding on to the edge of the mattress.

"I'm sorry," I say. "I was sick."

He shakes his head.

"You need to purify yourself. Come with me. We'll pray together."

"I need to go visit Christy in the hospital," I say as I walk, teetering, behind him.

"We'll see," he says. "You have lots of chores to do. Maybe this afternoon."

He opens the door to his musty-smelling room and we enter together.

Against the wall I notice my dad's shoes. Something in them catches the light from the hall and as my dad goes to light the candles, I look inside. My heart beats painfully loud in my chest. Broken glass and jagged stones are spread from one end to the other—spotted with dried brown blood like rust. The shock of seeing it is almost enough to knock the drugs out of my system—but not quite. My opiated daze keeps me from completely losing it.

"Come on," my dad says. "We have to subjugate ourselves before Him. We have to ask for His mercy."

I nod, but don't say anything.

I go and kneel next to my dad in front of the make-shift altar.

He clasps his hands in front of his face.

That gold ring with the coiled snakes is still on his finger.

The sight of it makes my stomach turn.

My father begins droning on and on.

I close my eyes and turn my head away.

But I can't escape.

A searing pain like fire beneath my skin makes me shiver and burn and a vision flashes in my mind.

The house becomes the house as it was before—the room becomes the room of the young boy. He kneels as we kneel now, holding the rosary beads in his clasped hands. He prays silently, but with his lips moving. His pale skin is like wax paper covering the delicate veins twisting beneath the surface.

A scream echoes through the house and the boy startles out of his reverie. The scream is followed by a heavy impact on the floor above him. Then there is the sound of footsteps running down the many flights of stairs. The footsteps are like a herd of cattle fleeing from the slaughter.

The boy rises up and goes quickly and quietly to the door.

He peers out, a hand covering his mouth.

The sisters, dressed in their nuns' habits, are hurrying down the stairs—some crying, some stumbling. Sister Angelica shouts at them from top floor, "Faster. Go. Faster."

Sister Margaret, her habit torn, tears streaming down her red, swollen face, limps down the stairs a little behind the others. And then Sister Angelica follows.

"It's time to repent," she says. "We must repent. We must be cleansed. We must ask for God's mercy."

She takes out a small Bible and begins to read, even as she descends the stairs. She reads from the book of Revelations.

"But the cowardly, the unbelieving, the vile, those who practice magic arts, the idolaters, and all liars—they will be consigned to the fiery lake of burning sulfur. This is the second death."

The boy creeps soundlessly down the hall. He keeps close to the railing, trying to make himself invisible. On the bottom floor the sisters all gather—speaking in hysterical whispers. Until Sister Angelica reaches them.

"This way," she says. "Come on, come on."

She goes to the basement door, pulling a long silver key out of the pocket of her robe, fitting it into the lock, and turning it so it clicks open.

She tells the sisters, "Down. Go down and be cleansed."

Then she begins to read again.

"And the great dragon was hurled down—that ancient serpent called the devil, who leads the whole world astray. He was hurled to the earth, and his angels with him."

The boy watches from the top of the stairs. He dares not follow.

Down in the basement candles are lit, casting shadows on the floor and ceiling.

Sister Angelica makes the sisters line up, one next to the other, facing the cracked, dirty concrete walls. She tells them to keep quiet—to keep their heads bowed. She tells them to pray for forgiveness. She paces back and forth, reading the Holy Scripture.

"And the devil, who deceived them, was thrown into a lake of burning sulfur, where the beast and false prophet had been thrown. They will be tormented day and night for all eternity."

Sister Margaret listens to the words, crying silently to herself—praying as best she can. But a sob escapes her lips and then Sister Angelica is there behind her. She turns ever so slightly to look. Sister Angelica takes her hair in her hand and shoves her face hard into the wall.

"I told you not to turn around," she says. "I told you to be quiet."

From out of the darkness the monsignor appears. He walks limping and bent a little at the waist. With one hand he grabs a candle from out of the holder, carrying it before him. The light from the flame makes the ruby sparkle on the gold ring with the two serpents on his finger.

As he approaches Sister Margaret, another girl, younger than the rest, her long, red hair pulled back tight beneath her habit, collapses on the cold cellar floor. No one moves to help her.

The monsignor stands behind Sister Margaret.

He speaks in a deep, rasping voice.

"Hold out your hand," he tells her.

Trembling, she does as she's told. She holds her small, elegant hand out to him. He takes it roughly in his own. As the sleeve of his hassock is pushed back, Sister Margaret notices a length of barbwire wrapped tightly around his arm, the barbed spikes cutting in so they draw blood.

The monsignor brings the candle up.

"Pray for forgiveness," he tells her.

Then he holds the flame to her open palm.

And no matter how she screams and cries and fights to get away, he keeps her held fast.

Until she releases a stream of burning urine down her leg.

And she falls to the ground, soaking and unconscious.

Coming out of the vision, I blink my eyes, trying to remember where I am. Turning to look, I see my dad still kneeling beside me. He reaches over, taking both my hands up and clasping them tightly.

"We are your servants, Lord," he says. "We shall do as you command. Thy will, not ours, be done."

He drops my hands and makes the sign of the cross over himself.

"In the name of the Father, the Son, and the Holy Ghost. . . . Amen.

"Amen," he repeats.

I feel dizzy and disoriented, but when he smiles at me, I try to smile back.

"Now," he says. "I'm not opposed to you visiting your friend in the hospital—and I want to get supplies for that storm coming in—but I need you to finish your chores first. Can you do that?"

"Of course," I tell him, my voice weak and quieter than I mean it to be.

I stand up then off the frayed rug—but looking down at my father, I see the imprint of something beneath his dress shirt. Is it my imagination, or are there small tears all over it? Is he wearing the string of barbwire, too? Feeling the sickness back in my stomach, I turn and run out of the room.

Downstairs I eat toast with strawberry jam and butter and drink strong coffee with milk and sugar.

I decide to call Stephanie back in Johnstown—to try to at least get some kind of outside perspective on all this craziness—even though I'm not too sure how to explain any of it.

Twisting the long phone cord over and over around my finger, I dial the number and wait to hear the familiar ringing. But no ringing comes. Instead, there is only a strange clicking and the sound of metallic breathing that makes the hackles all stand out on the back of my neck.

I slam the phone down.

I don't pick it up again.

Whatever that noise was—I don't want to hear it again.

So I forget trying to call her.

I guess she wouldn't understand any of this anyway.

It's pointless.

I leave the kitchen and the phone and set about doing my chores around the house. Then I put on boots and a heavy raincoat to go sweep the falling leaves outside. Already the gray clouds have turned black overhead. When I get right up on the perimeter of the forest, I duck quickly behind the trees, then run stumbling through the wet leaves and twisted roots.

I have to take the back roads into town, but eventually I make it to the little drugstore, where I buy five different pregnancy tests—just in case the first four don't give me the answer I'm looking for.

By the time I get back home, I realize it's almost time to meet Colin—if he shows up today. So I decide to wait on taking the pregnancy tests 'til after. I mean, obviously, if I find out I'm fucking pregnant *before* meeting him, that's all I'll be able to think about. If I wait, at least, I can stay in denial for a little while longer. When in doubt, stuff it way down deep inside and don't look at it again until it comes up and bites you in the ass. That's how you know I'm my father's daughter.

So I hide the pregnancy tests in that stone garage behind the house.

Then I walk back through the tall grass.

Entering the shadows of the forest, I hear a voice again whispering to me—familiar-sounding—like the older sister from my vision, Sister Angelica.

"Liar," it says. *"Sinner."*

I pass the giant oak with the initials carved into its trunk.

AMJG.

The voice like Sister Angelica's grows ever louder in my ears.

"The wicked shall be punished," it says. *"The wicked will burn."*

I shake my head, trying to clear it—trying to drown out the voices.

I walk deeper into the forest, crossing a small creek and sinking down into the mud. I take another step and then another. But then, in the impression of my boot print, something tied with a faded, now-colorless ribbon catches my eye. I bend to pick it up, only to recoil back in revulsion. It is a braid of thick, black hair, buried in the mud. Sickness almost overtakes me again, as I scramble out of the muddy creek bed into a covering of dead, rotting leaves.

I struggle to catch my breath.

And then I'm aware of a movement through the leaves—a rustling—something weaving there. I look down and have to cover my mouth to keep from screaming. A snake, fat and striped horizontally, with a big flat head and a rattle on its tail about an inch and a half long, comes gliding on the top of the leaves in a wide, sweeping S.

I step slowly backward out onto the grass.

A sour animal sweat breaks out all over my body. I feel it cold down my legs. My heart beats so hard and fast I can hardly catch my breath. I'm dizzy and dry-mouthed and I keep stepping backward and the snake keeps winding toward me. But then the snake stops its forward movement and it begins to coil in on itself. Its tail vibrates so fast it almost seems to be standing still. But I can hear the rattle. It sets my teeth on edge. The head of the snake weaves back and forth like a boxer. It gets ready to strike.

I close my eyes.

But I don't feel the bite.

On the grass in front of me I see the snake now, its head bashed open, with blood and brains and skin and I don't even know what splattered out across the dirt. I take a few more steps back and drop on my knees in the wet grass. Looking up, then, Colin is there holding a broken branch in one hand, breathing hard.

"Jesus Christ," he says. "That was close."

I run to him, before I can stop myself, wrapping my arms around him and bursting into tears.

"Hey, hey, it's all right. You're all right."

"I was so scared," I say, sobbing.

"Shh," he tells me. "You're okay."

He kisses the top of my head.

I don't pull away from him.

I look up at him smiling broadly down at me.

"You're all right," he says again.

I nod.

"Yeah, thank you."

And then I laugh, saying, "Jesus Christ. That was crazy."

"Yeah," he says. "I thought all the snakes were asleep this time of year."

"Me, too," I say.

I breathe out.

"I wasn't sure you were gonna come," I tell him. "I thought maybe because of the storm . . ."

He smiles.

"I wanted to check up on you," he says. "I heard about what happened with Christy."

I breathe in. "News travels fast, huh?"

He nods.

"There are a lot of secrets in this town," he says. "Only everyone knows them."

I chew on the inside of my cheek.

"Like what happened in Harmony House?" I ask.

"No," he says, looking off in the distance. "Those are secrets no one wants to know."

"Yeah, I understand why."

He narrows his eyes at me.

"What do you mean?" he asks.

I shrug.

"I don't know. Nothing. It's just these dreams I've been having. Dreams about the house, about the way it was."

"What do you mean?" he says, dropping his smile.

"I don't know," I say. "They seem so real. Like I'm seeing things that really happened there."

"Maybe you are."

I laugh.

"You don't think that's totally crazy?"

"No, not at all. A lot of terrible things happened in that house—things so terrible they can't ever go away."

"Great," I say, making a face at him. "And lucky me gets to live there."

He lets his shoulders rise and fall.

"Maybe this storm will come and wash it all away."

I laugh again.

"God, you sound like my dad."

"I do?"

I shake my head.

"No, not really. He just said something similar."

I stare down at nothing there in front of me before continuing on.

"It would be the best thing, though, wouldn't it?"

"Yeah," says Colin. "It would."

Looking around me, then, I realize that we've been walking this whole time back through the grown-close-together trees and tangled foliage. The darkening sky smells sweetly of rain and the wind seems to blow in a thousand directions at one. The branches bend, moaning pitifully.

At the edge of the forest we stop, Colin standing close to me, smiling, his eyes pained and beautifully sensitive.

"You probably have to get back," he says, still smiling.

"Yeah," I say. "Probably."

"Are you gonna go to the hospital to visit Christy?"

I nod.

"Yeah, for sure."

My hair is wet from the leaves overhead, but with Colin here close to me, I don't feel the cold.

"I'll come by later," he says. "To make sure you're all right."

"I'd like that," I say, and then quickly add, "Thank you for being so great to me."

He smiles big.

"Thank *you*," he says.

I think I must blush a little.

"You are seriously the only good thing in a really shitty day," I tell him.

"Good," he says. "That's what I want. I want to help you."

I laugh.

"I need a lot of it."

He shakes his head.

"No, you don't. You don't need help. But until you believe that for yourself, I'll be here."

I laugh again. "That's kind of cheesy, isn't it?"

"Maybe it is," he says, shrugging. "But it's true."

"You're sweet," I tell him.

And then, before I can stop myself, I lean forward and I kiss his soft mouth and he kisses me and I feel weightless—almost lifted off the ground. But then I remember the pregnancy tests hidden in the back garage. The shame cuts down along the curve of my belly, spilling out my insides. I pull away from him.

"I'm sorry," I say. "I want this. I do. But everything is way too fucked up right now."

Colin smiles warmly—with complete patience and understanding.

"I'm here for you," he says.

And it almost makes me want to cry.

I kiss him again, but quickly now, on the cheek.

"Thank you," I say again.

He nods and smiles.

And then I step out onto the wet grass behind the big, looming house. I make a wide semicircle first to the driveway and then double back to the stone garage. I get the plastic bag full of the many pregnancy tests and hide them under my jacket. Then, picking up the rake I hid, I walk around to the front of the house.

My dad is there unloading boxes from the back of his station wagon. Next to him, Sheriff Jarrett stands talking. When they see me, though, they both stop what they're doing.

"Where were you?" my dad asks. "I went into town to get some supplies, but I couldn't find you anywhere."

I come up a little closer and Sheriff Jarrett smiles real wide at me. He has a plug of chewing tobacco in his lip and is spitting into an empty soda can.

"I was raking leaves in the back," I say. "Just like you told me to."

The sheriff laughs pleasantly.

"Not a lot of point in raking leaves now," he says. "This storm's about to make a real mess 'a this whole town."

Turning to my dad, I say, "I thought you were going to wait and get supplies when we went to visit Christy in the hospital."

My dad shrugs.

"Yeah, well, I had some things I need to take care of."

"She's okay," the sheriff says. "They set her legs and her wrist. She's in and out of consciousness."

"What'd she say about what happened?" I ask.

The sheriff spits and shakes his head.

"Damnedest thing. She says she don't remember any of it."

"What do you mean?" I ask.

"She don't remember any of it. She didn't even remember coming over here last night."

I make a face.

"She doesn't remember anything?"

Again, he shakes his head.

"What about Candace and Mercedes?"

He leans back against the cruiser and scratches at the stubble on his chin.

"They're okay. Shaken up a little. That's all."

My dad hoists another box down out of the trunk of his car.

"I really do want to go see her," I say. "I feel awful about it."

The sheriff shakes his head.

"Now, now. It wasn't your fault."

My dad turns to him now.

"Well, then, Sheriff," he says. "It was very nice of you to check in on us. But, as you can see, we're doing just fine. I got all the supplies here for the storm. And if Jen does her work today, I wouldn't be opposed to her borrowing the car to go visit her friend."

Sheriff Jarrett smiles at him.

"Good, that's good. That's a good idea."

He looks at me and nods his head.

"It's real easy to get there," he says. "You just go straight on down that main road about twenty miles and it's right at the junction of Highway 17."

"Thank you," I say.

He tells me, "Don't mention it."

He gets into his cruiser and waves at both of us.

I go over to where my dad is standing and take up one of the boxes full of bottled water, canned goods, flashlights, and batteries. I struggle against its weight but manage to get it up the stairs and into the front hallway. I check to make sure my dad isn't following behind me. Then I go up to my room. And I get myself ready to go pee on some goddamn pregnancy tests.

CHAPTER 13

Locked in the upstairs bathroom staring at all five pregnancy tests with the two pink lines clearly visible meaning I am, in fact, FUCKING PREGNANT, my first thought is to go call Stephanie and ask for her help. But how can I even begin to explain all this to her? Alex breaking in, the voices, the dreams or visions or whatever they are, Christy jumping off the balcony, my dad wearing the monsignor's gold ring, him walking around with glass and rocks in his shoes—and maybe barbwire tied around his chest? It's all too much. Being here, living through it, I still can barely believe half of what's happened so far. Stephanie seems as far away from me as if I left Johnstown a hundred years ago.

I'm alone with this just like I'm alone with everything else.

I find myself wishing that my mom could be here. She'd understand, I think. I'd be able to talk to her. At least I wouldn't be so all alone.

As it is, I don't know what the hell to do.

All I can think of is that I need to get some money somehow and find a doctor. Looking back on all of this—how I got myself in this situation—none of it makes any sense. Before I came to Harmony House, the things I thought and cared about were so simple. Now nothing is.

So I find a spot under the sink, back behind some old cleaning products and rags, to hide the used tests. Then I wash my hands in burning-hot water—forcing myself not to pull away as the skin turns red and the pain shoots up and down my arm. Steam rises up out of the washbasin, clouding the mirror, filling the tiny bathroom. Through the steam a vision comes to me. As the water runs, I close my eyes and through the scalding pain, I see this same bathroom half a century ago.

I see the showerhead spraying water down into the claw-foot tub.

Sunlight shines in through the window.

Birds sing in the surrounding treetops. The morning dew on a spiderweb catches the light and reflects like a cluster of burning stars.

An infant cries from somewhere not far off.

Beneath the steady stream of water steaming in the small white-painted bathroom Sister Margaret stands—her long, beautiful hair wet down her back.

She scrubs with a cloth at the skin of her thighs and belly. She lathers the soap and washes beneath her arms. Her skin is the palest, most delicate, perfect, unblemished white. Or it would be, if not for the raised, blistering, crisscross of welts along her calves and up the backs of her legs.

As she cleans herself, her hand carefully avoids these tender places. She shies away from them as though they were hot to the touch, like an open flame.

But still, she soaks up the water and feels the pleasure and warmth of it. She even sings to herself, though this is strictly forbidden. So she sings softly—a song she heard on the radio once and she has kept as a secret for herself to be sung only in these private moments, away from spying ears.

She mouths the words quietly.

"I . . . fall . . . to pieces . . . each time someone speaks . . . your name. I . . . fall . . . to pieces . . . time only adds to the flame."

She smiles as she sings and, for now, she is happy here— safe and alone.

Except that she is not alone.

The steam filling the bathroom escapes from the tiniest crack in the bathroom door.

Out in the hall, the little boy—the quiet, shy little boy— crouches with his eye to the keyhole. He watches with the most painful, aching longing. Guilt and desire wrack his young body. He trembles, just wanting to take her away from all this—to free her—to run far away and never look back.

And then, from behind him, a voice calls out. It is the hoarse, ugly, vile croaking of the older nun—Sister Angelica.

"What do you think you're doing?" she shouts, grabbing him by the shoulder and wrenching him around.

She stares down at him, looking his whole body over.

"Aw, Lord protect us," she says. "You are disgusting."

The boy's body vibrates with terror. His hands shake. His mouth quivers.

"Just look at yourself," she says, almost smiling now— showing off her brown-stained, yellow teeth.

The boy tries to speak, but no words come out.

"Sick," she says. "Sick. You wait 'til Father Meyers hears about this."

Sound comes from the boy's mouth now.

"P-please," he says. "No."

"Well, then how about I tell Sister Margaret? I'm sure she'd love to know how her star pupil lusts of the flesh after her."

"No, please," he cries again, his voice even more tremulous with panic. "It's not like that. She's pure and holy. She's more pure than anything."

The old nun laughs cruelly.

"Get up against the wall," she says.

"What?" the boy asks, with tears coming down now.

"Do as I say," the old woman sneers. "Up against the wall. Face away from me."

The boy does as he's told. He presses his face and body up against the wall.

The old nun takes a steel ruler from behind her back, the edge sharpened to make almost a knife's point.

"For every lash," she tells him, her voice calmer now, "you will say one Hail Mary and one Our Father. Is that understood?"

The boy cries, pressing himself in against the cold wall.

"I said, is that understood?"

The boy nods, snot running down his nose.

"Then we shall begin," the nun says.

She draws back her hand and, with a quick flick of her wrist, flays the skin of the boy's legs and buttocks.

"Hail Mary, full of grace," he starts to say.

But through the wall he can still hear Sister Margaret. She's still singing that same song.

"I . . . fall . . . to pieces."

Her voice is quiet—almost inaudible—but somehow more beautiful than anything the boy's ever heard in his whole life. The sound of her voice seems to call to him. He feels it stirring him—giving him strength.

The old nun whips the ruler against his backside again and he cries.

"Hail Mary, full of grace."

She hits him again.

And then again.

And again.

But he doesn't feel the pain of it.

He listens to Sister Margaret's voice.

The steel ruler tears the flesh from his bones.

Sister Margaret sings like a whispered dream of ecstasy.

The ruler draws blood, dripping in strange and delicate

patterns down his legs.

Sister Margaret sings.

And the skin is ripped away.

Until his body can take no more.

And he collapses on the ground.

As I come out of the dream, the water has gone cold from the faucet and is spilling out onto the cracked tile. I turn it off quickly and cover my face with my hands. I have to get these images out of my head, I think. I have to blot it all out.

Going back to my room, I take two more of the pills I think are Xanax. My supply is getting pretty low, which is the last thing I need, but there's nothing I can do about it. Stephanie and her mom are supposed to be coming for Thanksgiving. But already something tells me that's not going to happen. I'm so disconnected from the world here. I don't feel like I could ever be part of it again.

Of course, I could try to convince my dad to pack up and leave, but he seems like he's as much a part of this house now as all the rest of it.

"Well," I say out loud to myself. "At least I can get out of here for a little while."

Something slams into the window then, and I jump back, putting my hand to my chest.

There's a crack splintering across the glass.

I swallow down the panic and walk, carefully, over to the broken window.

On the ground in a clearing of tall grass, a grotesquely fat black crow lies with its neck broken.

I turn, sickened.

I drop down on the ground, the air all knocked out of my lungs.

"Why is all this happening to me?" I ask no one.

And no one answers.

I walk down the stairs to my dad's room, hoping to ask him for the keys to his car so I can go visit Christy in the hospital.

As I get closer, though, I hear what sounds like a low, sorrowful moan from behind his door, which has been left slightly ajar.

Trying to be quiet now, I look into the dark room, lit only with the flickering, warm glow of candles. A sickness crawls down my throat and into my stomach and I feel cold and like my heart's beating way too fucking loud.

My dad sits on a stool facing the wall.

I make out the bright shock of blood crisscrossing the pale white of his back. He holds a braided leather whip in his thick hands. He lashes at his back—over and over, again and again. The whip tears through his skin and raises wide, purple welts in lined patterns.

He winces from the pain and cries out, almost dropping the whip but recovering.

Around his torso and then again, diagonally, around his shoulder, the twisting strands of barbwire are tied tightly—cutting into his flesh.

On his hand the red ruby at the center of the monsignor's ring catches the flickering candlelight.

"*Mea culpa,*" he whispers. "*Mea culpa, mea culpa.*"

I take a step back from the door.

The whip lashes.

His voice echoes: "*Mea culpa, mea culpa.*"

I back up against the banister.

My dad cries out.

And I don't say anything at all.

I turn and run.

I get the keys from out of the bowl on the table in the front entranceway.

I go out into the storm winds—big droplets of rain now fall sporadically.

I turn the key in the ignition of the station wagon and switch the windshield wipers on.

I don't drive off right away.

I sit there breathing and feeling sick.

Please, I think, please, someone, I need some help.

But no help comes.

I am still alone.

And so I start to drive.

Because I don't know what else to do.

CHAPTER 14

When I pull up to the Staffordshire Township Hospital, a shiver runs through me—I remember now that this is where they brought Alex that night. My stomach tightens a little, wondering if he's still here.

Regardless, I need to see Christy and make sure she's okay. Of course, it wasn't my fault that she fell—or jumped. But I can't help but feel guilty somehow. It was my fault she was at Harmony House, after all.

So I get out of the car, hurrying because of the rain starting to fall. I enter through the automatic sliding glass door and cross to the reception desk. The woman behind the counter, rail thin, with big bug eyes and dark hair parted in the middle, directs me to the third floor.

The elevator is a long time coming and I look absently around at the doctors and nurses and orderlies walking purposefully up and down the hallway.

On the third floor, I hear the rain spattering the windows and smell that noxious hospital smell of disinfectants and cleaning products. The rubber soles of my boots squeak-squeak on the polished linoleum.

Christy's room is all the way down at the end of the hall. I knock twice quickly on the door and take a deep breath before going in.

It's a shock seeing Christy. Her entire body is wrapped tightly in different casts and bandages. Her left leg is elevated and her neck is in a brace. Both her eyes are swollen, bordered by black-and-blue marks like she's been punched in the face.

The breath I took in, I let out all at once.

"Jen," a voice says, scaring me so I jump back.

But, turning, I see it's only Rose. She's wearing a heavy barn coat and dirty jeans and she stands and comes over to hug me for a long time.

"Jen," she says again. "I'm so happy you're here. I

need to talk to you."

"I'm sorry," I tell her. "I feel so bad about Christy."

"There was nothing you could do," she says—holding me at arm's length now. "It's not your fault."

"I don't know how it happened," I say, feeling tears well in my eyes now.

"It's okay," she says again. "But I do want to talk to you. Do you mind coming out in the hall with me?"

I look over at Christy lying there.

"Of course," I say.

She smiles more and puts a hand on my shoulder.

I follow her out into the hall.

I lean back against the white-painted drywall, banging my head and then banging it again rhythmically—not too hard, but not too soft either.

"The storm's looking pretty bad," I say, just to say something.

She nods.

"It is going to be bad," she says. "That's something I wanted to talk to you about."

"About the storm?" I ask, making a face.

"Jen," she says. "I know this is going to sound a little . . . forward . . . but I'm very worried about you."

"I'm worried about myself," I tell her.

"With everything that's been happening at the house," she says, "I think it might be best for you to leave as soon as possible."

She's staring hard at me and I shiver.

"You mean because of Christy?" I ask.

"Because of that, yes. And Alex Winter. And the storm and, honestly, sweetie, you look sick—you're covered in bruises, you have dark circles under your eyes, you're thin and pale."

"Gee, thanks," I say. I actually laugh a little at that.

"You're a strong girl," she tells me, again putting her hand on my shoulder. "But you're not strong enough—not yet. And now this storm is coming. If I had some time with you, maybe I could teach you how to control the power you have, but as it is, I'm afraid you're in a lot of danger."

I laugh again, but there are still tears in my eyes.

"Power?" I say, incredulously. "I don't have any power. I'm totally powerless."

"No, you're not."

I move away from her then—not abruptly, but just to keep her from touching me.

"Look," I say. "I appreciate you trying to help. And I am sorry about what happened. But you don't know me.

I'm sorry, but you don't. You don't have any idea what's going on in my life."

She nods, smiling.

"I do know," she says. "I know because we're alike— because we're not like other people."

I breathe in and out.

"What?" I say, getting annoyed now. "Because you're a medium or something? Because you can read people?"

Again she nods. "Yes, I can read people. And yes, I'm a medium. But that's not what you are. You are something much, much more—"

I don't let her finish.

"Sorry," I say, the heat searing through me again. "I've got enough crazy shit to deal with in my life right now. I've got enough crazy fucking people."

I start to walk away from her. I press the palms of my hands into either side of my head and the heat is burning me alive.

"I know about the dreams," she says, calling after me. "I know about the visions. And I know about your father, too. You have to get out of that house. You have to leave tonight. If your father will come with you, then fine, but even if he refuses, you must get out tonight."

I turn back to face her, my vision blurred from the

heat consuming me. I feel like if I open my mouth I will spit fire. But only words come out.

"Where the hell am I supposed to go?" I yell, not caring who in the hospital hears me now.

She answers calmly.

"Go anywhere," she says. "Come to the diner. You can stay with me. You can stay with me right now, if you want."

She takes a step toward me, reaching out a hand.

"Stop it!" I yell even louder. "I can't stand it!"

And then there is a piteous groan from the building's foundation. The linoleum floor ripples like a swell coming in off the ocean. The whole building seems to jerk and shake. The walls rattle. One of the nurses from down the hall shouts, "Earthquake."

I go on and run to the stairs with the red glowing EXIT sign and start down them, even as the loud rumbling and shaking go on and on. As I reach the bottom floor, the building goes still again and the change of movement makes me almost trip over my own feet, but I catch myself on the landing and start out through the main lobby, where everyone is scrambling in a million directions at once. I step through the automatic sliding glass doors. The rain is falling steadily now. The sky is all black.

I drive slowly, trying not to think about Rose and everything she said—though, I guess, I can't help it.

Branches bend and break and the gutters overflow with leaves on either side of the road.

The sound of the windshield wipers is like my heart beating.

Rose's words keep repeating over and over in my mind.

She knew about the visions. She knew about the dreams. She said she knew about my father.

And she's right, of course—I have to get out of the house. I have to get out as soon as possible. And if my dad won't come with me . . . I guess I'll have to go without him. Not to Rose's. That's crazy. Maybe to Stephanie's.

Jesus Christ.

I really don't have anywhere to go.

But I have to go. I have to go somewhere.

As I pass through town I can just make out the boarded-up doors and taped shop windows and a few cars parked at the curb. The lights from the diner are still on—the neon sign a blur through the falling rain.

I make a decision then.

I'm going to ask my dad, once, to leave with me. I'm

going to give him a chance. If he says no, I'm going to get my stuff, get in the car, and go. If he tries to stop me, I'll call that sheriff. He'll help me. I know he will.

I pass through the gates leading up to the house. The rain beats mercilessly against the car roof and windshield. The sound is like perpetual thunder. The sound is like the earthquake. I round the corner so the dimmest outline of light from the monstrous house comes into view. A chill runs through me. Then I see that one of the big oak trees has fallen halfway across the road. I swerve and the car accelerates as if on its own, back tires spinning so I career off the embankment—hitting the front end hard so my neck snaps back and I slam sideways into the steering wheel. I taste blood in my mouth and my eyes start to close.

CHAPTER 15

Someone is there banging against the passenger window—banging louder even than the rain. My eyes adjust to the light—or absence of light. The door opens and the water washes in and the sound of the wind is like a river. But then I hear a voice and there are hands grabbing hold of my wet clothes and pulling me free.

It's Colin.

I wrap my arms around him and he says, "Okay, I got you." And he lifts me out onto the road. My legs feel weak beneath me and I'm dizzy and trembling.

"Come on, this way," he says.

He leads me stumbling through the forest—the trees all creaking and splitting and sounding like they're about to come down all around us.

"Hurry," he says.

And so we start to run now—coming out onto the driveway.

"I can't go home," I tell him.

He nods.

"It's okay," he says.

We go back to the stone garage and he opens a side door and we both run inside.

Thank God, it's at least pretty dry in here, though we're both still totally soaking wet. The garage seems like it must've been a converted barn, because there's an upper hayloft with horse blankets and wooden crates full of equipment. Colin finds an old oil lamp with a blown colored-glass chimney and a brass burner. He takes a silver-plated Zippo from his coat pocket and lights the wick. It catches immediately and he adjusts the flame and then I can see his features more defined again. He sets the lamp down on a wooden crate and shakes his head at me.

"You're a real mess, you know that?" he says.

In spite of everything, I laugh.

"Tell me about it."

I unfold one of the heavy wool blankets and wrap it around myself, then climb up the broken and splintered-in-places ladder to the sweet-smelling hayloft. Around us the storm rages. Inside we are warm and safe-feeling, and I breathe out.

Colin climbs up next to me, carrying more of the heavy blankets.

"You think your dad's gonna come looking for you?" he asks.

I shrug and pull the blanket tighter around me.

"At this point," I say, "I don't even care."

I start unlacing my boots.

"Hey," I say. "What were you doing here, anyway? Shouldn't you be home with your family?"

He shakes his head.

"They're fine. You're the one I was worried about. I wanted to come check up on you."

"I'm glad you did," I say. "Jesus Christ, I'm glad you did."

I get my boots and socks off and bury my bare feet in the straw.

"How long's this storm supposed to last?" I ask him.

He runs a hand across his head.

"How long do you want it to be?"

I manage to laugh a little.

"As long as we're in here and not the house and I don't have to deal with my dad, it can last forever, as far as I care."

"Did you go see Christy?" he asks, leaning back against the moss-covered wall. He has one blanket over his shoulders and another is laid out covering the both of us.

"I tried," I say. "She was unconscious. She looked terrible."

Colin shakes his head.

"I'm sorry," he says.

"I did get to talk to Rose, though," I tell him. "That was a lot of fun."

He laughs a little. "Do I sense a little sarcasm there?"

"Very perceptive, yeah. She's kind of a whack job, isn't she?"

He shrugs. "Well, like I said, she's known around town for being able to talk to dead people, so . . ."

He pauses then before continuing on, asking, "Is that what you mean?"

I laugh a little more.

"I guess so. I don't know. I kind of lost it on her, to tell you the truth."

He laughs, too.

"Lost it how?"

"I think I was just sick of everything being so crazy, I kind of took it out on her."

"What did she say to you?"

I let my shoulders rise and fall.

"Just that I wasn't safe in the house. That I had to get out. Which is kind of like, duh, I guess. But she also said she knew about the dreams, or the visions, or whatever. Oh, and that she knew about my dad, whatever that means."

"What about him?"

"She didn't say. Or . . . well . . . I didn't give her time to, maybe. She said I was, like, powerful, or something. That I had some power in me, or . . . I don't know. I guess that's what pissed me off so much."

He smiles and shakes his head.

"You got pissed off 'cause she said you're powerful?"

I smile along with him.

"Pretty dumb, huh?"

I bite my thumbnail. "It was more than that, though. It was like she was saying I'm some kind of . . . freak. Or . . . like . . . it was my fault, 'cause I could control it."

"Control what?"

"I don't know. Maybe that's not what she said. But it was something like that."

He reaches his hand out from under the blanket then and takes hold of mine. The warmth of him makes my heart beat fast again.

"Sounds to me," he says, "like she sees something pretty great in you."

He squeezes my hand and I smile.

"Then her skills as a psychic," I say, "are definitely lacking."

"I think you're pretty great," he says.

I blush at that.

"You don't know me," I tell him.

His body moves down closer to mine and I hold my breath. I realize I'm praying over and over again that he doesn't ruin this by trying to kiss me. But, for now, at least, he doesn't. He lies down on his back next to me staring up at the crossbeams in the ceiling.

"I'm sorry things have been so hard," he tells me.

It surprises me.

And I actually almost start to cry.

"It's really been one fucked-up thing after another," I tell him.

"I know," he says.

"Jesus, I mean, if I had any power, I sure as hell wouldn't be in this fucked-up situation now, would I?"

His hand finds mine again and again he squeezes it, but gently.

"Maybe you haven't found it yet."

I make a face.

"Found what?"

"Your power."

"Yeah," I say. "And maybe it isn't there."

He turns on his side, facing me.

"Maybe you keep running away from it."

A flash of memory makes me stumble over the words as I try to answer him.

My mom and dad had gotten into a fight, I guess—I don't know what about. I just remember sitting in front of the TV, watching a movie, and the more they fought, the more they screamed and screamed at each other— more and more high-pitched and piercing—the louder I turned the volume on the TV.

And then my mom came into the room and her face was red and streaked with makeup and her eyes were swollen and her hair a mess. I turned to look and her and then looked back at the TV with the volume loud so I didn't have to know or see—so I could be left alone—so

I could run away—escape into the movie—Clint East-wood throwing back his tattered poncho, revealing, as if by magic, the gun in his hand—fanning the hammer.

My mom came and grabbed my arm and yanked me to my feet.

"I'm watching this," I said.

And she told me, "Come on, we're leaving."

And I wanted to stay—or I thought if I did leave that my dad would think I was choosing her over him, that I was betraying him somehow.

"Mom, no!" I said. "No!"

"You're coming with me!" she said.

She dragged me, still by the arm, out of the house and put me in the passenger seat and buckled me in and fired the engine, and we started off down the driveway. It was night and the only lights were from the windows of the surrounding houses.

My dad came out of the darkness, throwing himself at the car and yelling, "Stop! Stop!"

But my mom kept on driving and he was thrown back against the white picket fence surrounding the dead-grass front yard.

"Mom!" I shouted, covering my face with my hands.

But I did not cry.

We drove fast down the block—tires screeching loud as we took the corner and fishtailed across the center divide. My mom had her foot pressed all the way to the floor and it sounded like the engine was going to break apart into a thousand pieces at any second.

But then we were pulling into a parking lot and my mom had the car in park, but still running, and she grabbed her purse and walked quickly toward the blinking-on-and-off neon sign of the liquor store—leaving the driver's-side door open.

She returned in what seemed like an instant—like I'd closed my eyes and opened them and then she was back, the outline of a bottle clearly visible beneath the brown paper bag clutched tightly in her hand. She unscrewed the cap.

"Mom!" I said. "Mom, no!"

Her eyes fixed on mine and for some reason, in that moment, I didn't look away. I stared back and I could see the pupils huge and darting in the darkness and the swallowing black inside her—like a dark star pulling everything into it, but never being filled.

"Mom, stop!" I yelled, not even knowing exactly why. Seeing the sickness so defined in her—seeing the coiled parasite like a tapeworm in the loops of her intestines, digesting and stealing and growing ever more powerful while she grew ever weaker.

She brought the bottle to her lips.

She tilted her head back.

"Mom! No!" I yelled—my eyes fixed on her—my eyes unable to turn away.

"Mom!" I screamed.

And in an intake of breath the bottle in the brown paper bag shattered in her hand. The glass turned to tiny sparkling glittering shards and liquid exploded out, tearing the bag and showering down with the glass onto the cracked and uneven asphalt. My mother's hand was cut and bleeding. Tears ran down her cheeks. She looked up at me. She held her bleeding palm up for me to see.

"You did this!" she said. "You did!"

I opened the car door then and got down onto the ground, but not feeling my legs beneath me as I started to run and run and run—back to the house—away from her—away from what happened—whatever it was. Only I knew one thing—I knew that it wasn't me, that I hadn't done it, that it wasn't my fault.

Except that it happened. It wasn't a dream. It was a memory.

And I remember it.

For the first time.

I blink my eyes back to the present—back here with Colin.

"I don't have any power," I say, telling him the truth. "Please, let's just drop this stupid conversation."

He leans forward, too quick for me to stop him, and kisses me on the temple. Then he lies back.

"You're right," he says. "I'm sorry."

"No, I'm sorry," I say. "You've been nothing but good to me. I guess I have a hard time with that sometimes."

He nods.

He doesn't say anything.

He pushes my hair back out of my eyes, gently still.

"I'm not a good person," I say.

"Shh," he tells me. "That's not true. I see who you are."

"No," I say. "You don't. No one does."

He smiles.

"Maybe that's the problem."

"Believe me," I say. "If you could see inside me, you'd run as far away from me as you possibly could."

"That's a lie you tell yourself," he says. "You're beautiful."

"I'm disgusting," I say.

He says, "Shh, shh."

He runs his hand through my hair.

He kisses my forehead.

"What happened to you?" he asks, whispering. "To make you hate yourself so much, when you are such an extraordinary person?"

My eyes spill over with tears again.

"I don't want to be extraordinary," I tell him. "I just want to be ordinary. I just want to be like everybody else."

He wipes my tears away.

"You never will be," he says. "I wouldn't be here, if you were."

I laugh then through my crying.

"You're trapped here because of the storm."

He kisses my tears now.

"I wouldn't want to be anywhere else," he says.

I feel myself becoming weightless from his kisses.

But I try to bring myself back down, saying, "Well, that's just stupid. We could still be together. But how about on a beach in Tahiti instead of the leaking garage?"

"No," he says. "I only want to be right here, with you, right now."

He kisses me again.

I kiss back.

We lie together like that.

We lie together 'til the lamplight burns down to black.

Until the walls come crashing down around us.

And the ocean rushes in.

And we hold the sun frozen in our bellies.

And in our happiness, we sleep.

And in our sleep, we dream.

We dream of each other.

Or, at least, I dream of him.

And in the dream I see the house.

But run-down-looking.

With boarded up windows and paint peeling off the sides and the roof caved in. The sun is setting low over the distant treetops.

Crickets chirp loudly in the tall grass. Clouds of mosquitos swarm the two boys walking around the perimeter. Colin wears the same rugby shirt and work pants. He's walking crouched down, creeping, along the side of the house. The boy with him is . . . Alex . . . that same Alex. Only he looks younger, somehow. His hair is shorter, sticking up in front.

The two boys find a broken window on the first floor. They look back and forth at each other. Then, cautiously, they climb inside—one after the other.

The room they enter is dark and dusty and smells like mold and some kind of dead animal rotting under the house. Furniture is piled haphazardly, covered in white sheets. Cobwebs hang from the corners of the ceilings. Desks and tables and dressers are piled on top of one another.

Walking with purpose, as though knowing exactly where they're going, the boys cross through the room and go out into the long hallway.

"I hope it's still here," Colin says, looking around.

Alex nods.

"Yeah. No one else comes in here. They're all too scared."

"I don't blame them," Colin says.

Alex narrows his eyes at him.

"Yeah, that's why you didn't take it last time."

"It just seems like it might be . . . I don't know . . . bad luck, or something."

Alex grins.

"Yeah, you told me. Well, you don't have to worry. I'll take it myself."

"How much you think you can get for it?"

Alex shakes his head.

"If it's solid gold, like you say, then it should be worth a lot."

They start up the big winding staircase, the banister gray

and greasy, with a thick layer of dust.

"I guess you're gonna want a cut, huh?" Alex asks.

Colin chews on his bottom lip.

"No, man. It's all you. This whole thing gives me the creeps."

Alex laughs.

The two boys climb the rest of the way in silence.

When they reach the top floor, they walk down the creaking, dirty hallway to the room next to the upstairs bathroom—the storage room. The windows are caked with dust and dried mud, so the bright sunlight is dulled to a soft glowing yellow—casting long shadows across the piled furniture and boxes and sheets draped over the old player piano, bench, and sheet music.

"It's in that desk drawer there," Colin says.

Alex smiles.

"Good."

He goes over to the rolltop desk and opens the side drawer. There among the black-and-white and color photographs is the monsignor's ring.

Alex takes it up in his hand.

"Looks like real gold to me. Feel how heavy it is."

He holds it out to Colin, but Colin backs away.

"Nah, man. I'm good."

Alex laughs again.

"Fine with me," he says.

He drops the ring in his front pants pocket.

"Let's look around and see what else we can find," he says.

A wave of nausea sweeps through Colin and he puts a hand over his mouth.

"I'm gonna be sick," he manages to say before running out of the room, where he vomits on his knees in the hall.

"Jesus, you are a sensitive little flower, aren't you?" he hears Alex say, laughing more.

Colin vomits again. He spits and vomits and clutches at his stomach.

"Ugh, I don't know what's wrong with me," he says finally.

He spits again and gets up.

He doesn't see Alex around, but goes to the next-door bathroom. Surprisingly, the water comes on when he turns the rusted faucet in the chipped and broken sink. He lets the brown, tepid water run for a minute before drinking from his cupped hands. Then he takes a pack of gum from his pocket, unwraps a piece, and pops it in his mouth. He breathes out.

"What the hell was that?" he says, out loud, to himself.

Stepping back out in the hall, he looks for Alex again but can't see him anywhere.

"Alex!" he calls, not too loud, because he doesn't want to make too much noise.

There's no response.

He looks back into the storage room, where he found the ring a week earlier and where now Alex has taken it for himself. The room is empty.

So Colin begins to search through the house, going back down to the second floor and calling out for Alex, but not finding him anywhere. A cold feeling creeps over the back of his neck and he is dizzy and weak, but still he keeps searching. He makes his way through the many rooms.

"Alex, this isn't funny, man," he calls.

But, again, there is no answer.

He descends the stairs to the basement. Light filters in through the dirt-caked, narrow windows. Dust motes are visible drifting and circling through the rays of light.

Down on the damp concrete cellar floor, boxes are stacked ceiling-high and wooden wine barrels are knocked over on their sides and busted open.

"Alex!" he tries again.

A voice whispers back this time.

"Sinner."

The word is spoken right in his ear.

"Jesus Christ," he says, going for the stairs now, ready to

just get the hell out of there.

But then Alex's silhouette fills the doorframe at the top of the stairs. In his hand he holds a metal fire poker, the handle worked into the shape of a snake, coiling.

"Where the hell'd you go, man?" Colin asks, trying to hide the tremor in his voice.

Still Alex doesn't answer. He raises the sharp, pointed metal rod up over his head, then he runs straight at Colin. He wields the poker and Colin steps back.

"What the hell?" he says lamely.

Alex brings the poker down and Colin is knocked to the floor. He holds his hand to his head, now wet and sticky with blood. Alex lets out a terrible, unearthly scream and brings the poker down again. But this time Colin is ready and he rolls out of the way. He leaps then at Alex, slamming his body into him and beating on him with his fists.

As Alex falls back, hitting the concrete, the ring—the monsignor's ring—flies from his pocket and bounces off into a dark corner of the basement. Colin lunges at Alex again. Alex swings the poker across his own body, and as Colin falls on top of Alex, he also falls on the poker, impaling himself on the sharp blade. The poker goes all the way through him, piercing his lung and exiting his back. Colin's weight is heavy as he tries to take a breath but can't get any air. Blood pumps in spurts out on the concrete with the beating of Colin's failing heart.

Alex pushes Colin off him and climbs back to his feet. He stares down at his friend, slowly dying there in front of him. Colin's mouth opens and closes.

It takes several minutes for the life to drain out of him. Alex watches, fascinated, all the while.

When Colin is dead, Alex wraps his body in a number of sheets, then drags him, sweating and out of breath, up the stairs, down the hallway, and out that same broken window they'd climbed into only an hour or so before.

He drags Colin's corpse through the tall grass and down the path and then deeper, still, into the forest. He covers his body in a blanket of dead leaves and a thin layer of dirt—the metal poker still protruding from his chest.

Alex leaves him, then, going back down the trail to the beach and the ocean beyond. He takes off his shirt and begins trying to wash the blood away in the cold salt water. Then he reaches into his pocket, as though suddenly remembering. Of course, the ring is not there. But he doesn't dare to go looking for it.

And so he makes his way back home.

While the body of his friend lies rotting in the forest.

CHAPTER 16

I wake with a crushing pain in my head.

The door to the garage is open and the wind sounds like a wounded animal caught in a trap. The oil lamp has burned out so there is only darkness illuminated by bright flashes of lightning. Thunder claps and makes the walls shake.

I sit up, holding my hand to my head, and try to look around, but I can't see Colin anywhere. I call to him.

"Colin!"

There is no answer.

And then I see the bent silhouetted frame of my father standing in the doorway. He walks in staggering, dragging his left leg. He holds something in his hand.

Lightning turns the sky a sickly pale white and his features appear gaunt and sneering. He keeps on walking toward me.

"Dad," I say, my voice shaky and uneven. "Dad. I'm sorry. I had an accident in the car. I came in here to get out of the storm."

My dad stops moving toward me and says, almost too quiet to hear over the rain and wind and thunder, "Get down here. Right now!"

I scramble to get my socks and boots on, then I climb quickly down the ladder.

"I'm sorry," I say again. "I just had to get out of the storm."

He raises his hand, showing me one of the positive pregnancy tests—shoving it in my face.

"I should've known," he says. "It was right in front of my face all this time."

"Dad," I plead. "That isn't mine."

He throws the test against the wall.

I watch it break and fall to the floor.

I feel my dad's hand gripping my arm.

It's like it could break.

I cry out.

And then he releases it.

"It's my fault," he says. "I should've seen. I should've known."

"It's not what you think," I say.

"The devil was in your mother," he tells me, speaking calmly now. "And now he's in you. He's been in you."

He grabs my arm again.

"But we will cast him out. Together, we will cast him out."

"Please, Dad," I say. "Please, you don't understand."

He pulls me toward him.

"I understand exactly. The devil's inside you. But I will take you to the house. You'll be rebaptized. I'll tear the devil out. We'll exorcise him from your soul."

The fire cuts through my brain again—raging through my insides. I clench my teeth together.

"Dad, no!" I say.

There's a clap of thunder that shakes the ground and I try to jerk my arm free, but my dad holds me fast.

"Don't fight me," he says. "The devil will try to fight, but you must resist him."

"Dad, you're sick," I tell him. "Please, you need help."

"That's the devil in you," he says. "He's got hold of you. You're burning in his eternal flame. The fire burns you from the inside out."

He pulls me toward the door and the rain and the wind and the lightning and thunder.

And it's true, I think, the fire is burning me alive.

"We will tear it from your heart and gouge out its eyes."

"Dad, please, let me go. Please. I didn't do anything wrong."

"You speak with the devil's tongue. You must be silent. Do not let his words corrupt your ears and defile you."

He drags me toward the door and I scream.

"Stop! Stop it!"

And then I call for help. "Somebody! Please! Colin! Colin!"

I try to wrench myself free. A blow hits me on the side of the head.

And I go down.

And there is only unconsciousness.

And in that unconsciousness, I see:

Winter in the darkness and the bare, frozen branches tap-tap against the fogged icy glass windows. Windblown snow paints

*the gray sky white. Within the cracked walls a fire offers lit-
tle heat, burning dully in the shallow hearth. An Oriental
rug frayed at the edges is laid out across the roughly textured
floorboards. The light is dim and flickering—shadowy—
playing across the face of the same small, pale-skinned boy
with inky blue-black hair and clear blue eyes. He wears a
white pressed shirt, wool pants, and jacket. His hands clasp a
leather-bound book and beaded rosary.*

*Kneeling next to him is Sister Margaret, again dressed in
a habit, with a cross dangling from her neck—the cross on a
silver chain reflecting yellow light.*

*The boy opens his eyes, looking up at her—thinking for
the thousandth time that she is the most beautiful person he's
ever seen. To him she is only pure and perfect.*

*He follows her down to the nursery—the walls painted a
washed-out pink trimmed with painted pink and white roses.
The curtains are drawn—the air cold and stale. The infants
take turns crying and kicking their legs and flailing their
arms uselessly—dressed in white lace nightgowns.*

*The boy follows Sister Margaret with a jar of silvery-gray
ashes as she makes the sign of the cross over each baby's tiny
forehead.*

*"In the name of the Father, the Son, and the Holy
Ghost. . . . Amen."*

Sister Margaret smiles down at him, her teeth white and

straight, her lips full. He watches her with his own eyes flashing. But then she tells him to wait while she goes to get fresh towels. She leaves. The boy walks to the window, looking out on the snowy wilderness. A bird, huge and black, smashes into the frozen glass. The boy jumps back, spilling the sacred ashes on the polished wood floor. He falls to his knees, panicking, holding his breath, desperately trying to get the spilled ashes back in the jar.

Someone shouts from just behind him—the voice of a man, deep and rasping. It is the monsignor.

The boy trembles violently as he approaches.

The monsignor's baritone bass voice booms out.

He holds a small leather whip in one hand.

He raises it high above his head.

The boy trembles and wets his pants.

The priest calls the boy's name.

Urine pools beneath the boy on the floor.

The priest says his name again.

"Anselm Noonan!"

Then the whip comes down.

CHAPTER 17

I am first aware of the cold concrete pressed against my cheek. My hair has fallen down in front of my eyes and a steady pressure at the back of my neck keeps me pinned where I am. That blood taste is back in my mouth and I have to be sick. I retch against the wall and I feel the pressure release.

Then I hear my father's voice. My father, the boy who lived here in Harmony House. The visions are coming on more and more frequently. I feel myself out of any one time—drifting from the past to the present.

But now I am down in the basement, held fast against the wall the way the sisters of Harmony House were. My dad stands holding a silver cross and rosary, like the monsignor did. He wears the monsignor's ring. He speaks with his voice. On the ground, at his feet, are the torn pages of the book—the words all crossed out with thick black lines. Candles are lit. The flames make the long shadows writhe like snakes. Without the rain and wind and thunder claps and flashes of lightning make the whole world seem like it's going to come crashing down around me. I hear the falling of the trees in the forest.

And through it all my father's voice like the monsignor's carries through the echoing basement. Reverberating so it seems to berate me on all sides— like the monsignor's whip lashing. Like Sister Angelica's edged metal ruler. I feel the stinging pain of his words like there really is a devil in me that's clinging on for possession.

"Lord have mercy," my father says.

> "Christ have mercy. Holy Mother of God,
> Holy Virgin of virgins,
> Saint Michael,

Saint Gabriel,
Saint Raphael,
All holy *angels* and archangels,
All *holy orders* of blessed spirits,

"From all evil, deliver us, Oh Lord.
From all sin,
From your wrath,
From sudden and unprovided death,
From the snares of the devil,
From anger, hatred, and all ill will,
By your coming,
By your birth,

"By *your cross* and passion,
By your holy resurrection,
By your wondrous ascension,

"Strike terror, Lord, into the beast now laying waste your vineyard. Fill your servants with courage to fight manfully against that reprobate dragon, lest he despise those who put their trust in you, and say with Pharaoh of old: 'I know not God, nor *will* I set Israel free.'

"Let your mighty hand cast him out of your servant,

Jennifer Noonan, so he may no longer hold captive this *person* whom it pleased you to make in your image, and to redeem through your Son; who lives and reigns with you, in the *unity* of the Holy Spirit, God, forever and ever."

"Dad," I whimper. "Dad, please. Don't do this."

A pain shoots through me then as if a bite has been taken out of my side and I can't help but cry out and put my hand to the tender skin there and fall to my knees.

"I command you, unclean spirit," my father shouts. "Whoever you are, along with all your minions now attacking this servant of God, by the mysteries of the incarnation, passion, resurrection, and *ascension* of our *Lord Jesus* Christ, by the descent of the Holy Spirit, by the coming of our *Lord* for judgment, that you tell me by some sign your name, and the day and hour of your departure.

"I command you, moreover, to obey me to the letter, I who am a *minister* of *God* despite my unworthiness; nor shall you be emboldened to harm in any way this creature of God, or the bystanders, or any of their possessions."

He lays his hand on the back of my head again and his touch is like a flame burning me, so I struggle to get away, though I'm too weak.

"Stop," I say. "Please. Dad, you need help. I can help you."

He goes on with his shouting prayer:

"When *time* began, the Word was there, and the Word was face-to-face with God, and the Word was God. This Word, when *time* began, was face-to-face with God. All things came into being through Him, and without Him there came to be not one thing that has come to be.

"In Him was life, and the *life* was the light of men. The light shines in the darkness, and the darkness did not lay hold of it. There came upon the scene a man, a messenger from God, whose name was John. This *man* came to give testimony to testify in behalf of the light that all might believe through him. He was not himself the light; he only was to testify in behalf of the light.

"Meanwhile the true light, which illumines every man, was making its entrance into the world. He was in the world, and the world came to be through Him, and the world did not acknowledge Him. He came into His home, and His own people did not welcome Him.

"But to as many as welcomed Him, He gave the power to become *children* of *God* those who believe in

His name; who were born not of blood, or of carnal desire, or of man's will; no, they were born of God. And the Word became 'man' and lived among us; and we have looked upon His *glory* such a *glory* as befits the Father's only begotten Son full of *grace* and truth!"

I'm lying fetal on the cold concrete floor now and my dad crosses himself and bends to kiss me on the forehead and I try to spit at him, shouting, "Fuck you!"

And his words cut into me like an axe blade:

"At that *time Jesus* was driving out a demon, and this particular *demon* was dumb. The *demon* was driven out, the dumb *man* spoke, and the crowds were enraptured.

"But some among the people remarked: 'He is a tool of Beelzebul, and that is how he drives out demons!' Another group, intending to test Him, demanded of Him a *proof* of His claims, to be shown in the sky. He knew their inmost thoughts. 'Any kingdom torn by civil strife,' He said to them, 'is laid in ruins; and house tumbles upon house.'

"'So, too, if *Satan* is in revolt against himself, how can his kingdom last, since you say that I drive out demons as a tool of Beelzebul. And furthermore: If I drive out demons as a tool of Beelzebul, whose tools are your pupils when they do the driving out?

"'Therefore, judged by them, you must stand condemned.

"'But, if, on the contrary, I drive out demons by the finger of God, then evidently the kingdom of *God* has by this *time* made its way to you. As long as a mighty *lord* in full armor guards his premises, he is in peaceful possession of his property; but should one mightier than he attack and overcome him, he *will* strip him of his armor, on which he had relied, and distribute the spoils taken from him.'"

He goes to kiss me again and I retch more, but nothing comes out. I feel something soaking through my jeans and look down to see blood pooling between my legs.

"Dad, please," I say. "Stop!"

And then I yell to anyone and no one.

"Somebody please help me! Please!"

My dad makes the sign of the cross above me again. He holds up the book of prayers with the pages torn out and says, beseeching,

"Almighty Lord, Word of *God* the Father, *Jesus* Christ, *God* and *Lord* of all creation; who gave to your holy *apostles* the power to tramp underfoot serpents and scorpions; who along with the other mandates to work miracles was pleased to grant them the authority to say: 'Depart, you devils!' and by whose might *Satan* was made to fall from *heaven* like lightning;

"I humbly call on your holy name in fear and trembling, asking that you grant me, your unworthy servant, pardon for all my sins, steadfast faith, and the power—supported by your mighty arm—to confront with confidence and resolution this cruel demon. I ask this through you, *Jesus* Christ, our *Lord* and God, who are coming to judge both the living and the dead and the world by fire."

And then there is a sound loud like the chiming of bells that cuts through the chaos around me. It comes again and again.

My dad lays down the book and the cross and the rosary and we both turn and look up to the stairs leading back to the main floor of the house.

The bells chime again.

And again.

It is the doorbell.

Someone is ringing the doorbell.

"Stay here," my father says. "Do not move."

He gets up from his place kneeling above me and crosses himself and goes to the stairs. I watch him climbing them slowly. He opens the door and closes it behind him. Then I hear a key turn in the lock and the bolt drawn.

Fuck.

I push myself up and feel the room spin around me and I start to black out—even as I crawl toward the steps. I see the vision as if it's being projected around me on the walls and ceiling.

In the vision I see the garden beyond the house. It is sum-mer—hot—a cool wind blowing in off the ocean. Birds sing overhead and squirrels chase one another through the trees and across the grass.

At the edge of the forest I see my father but as a young boy. I watch him watching Sister Margaret—who is waiting by the large, reaching-up oak tree where Anselm and the sister had that picnic together. But Anselm—the boy—and the sister are not together now. He watches her from afar—and she watches the forest. She watches and waits. The boy Anselm has dark circles under both eyes. He clenches his fists.

And then through the forest a man comes crashing through the underbrush. He is young and handsome, wear-ing a white T-shirt and paint-splattered jeans rolled up to the ankles and boat shoes. He's a local dockworker from the town. Sister Margaret smiles as the young man comes closer. Her whole face lights up and she flushes bright red. The young man smiles, too, his rugged face broad and handsome. They clasp hands and then he kisses her on the mouth. She kisses back.

The boy Anselm takes a step back.

Sister Margaret and the young man kiss and talk about their future. The young man laughs and pulls a switchblade out of his pocket. Still laughing and smiling, he carves their initials into the bark of the great tree. They are the same initials I saw carved into the tree that first day I moved into Harmony House. Only they are different. The initials I saw were AMJG. But what the young man carves in are only the two initials M and J. So he must be J. And M is Margaret.

They kiss again and hold each other close.

While the boy Anselm storms off. He's seen enough. Anger pulses through his whole body. He rages to himself.

She is a sinner, he thinks. She is just like all the rest.

He decides to tell the monsignor. He decides to tell him what Sister Margaret has done. Father Meyers will punish her. He will teach her a lesson. He will give Sister Margaret what she deserves.

The boy Anselm wants her to pay.

And so he betrays her to the monsignor.

And there is no going back.

Coming out of the vision, I find myself at the basement door.

I try the handle, but the lock holds fast.

There is nothing in me now but the blind need to get free—to get away from my dad and this craziness and to run and run and run and never stop.

I put my hand on the doorknob again.

A voice whispers in my ear.

Only it's not a voice.

It's a memory of a voice—Rose's words repeating over and over in my mind,

"If I had some time with you, maybe I could teach you how to control the power you have, but as it is, I'm afraid you're in a lot of danger."

The power I have?

What the hell does that mean?

And what did Colin say?

"Maybe you haven't found it yet."

But what was Colin anyway?

There's the heat in me like oil fire burning. It's like the fire is in my breathing. It goes from my lungs out my throat and mouth.

I try the door again.

It stays locked.

I mean, Jesus Christ, if I did have some power,

wouldn't I know about it? Other than having these visions that don't do me any good at all. If I have some power in me, then goddammit, I need to open this door.

The fire burns through my hands and out my fingertips.

I need this door to open now.

I need to get out of this house.

I have the power to see every fucking thing that's happened in this house.

Give me the power to get the hell out of here.

The fire burns my eyes and I have tears coming down.

I try the door.

I try the door again.

I try it again.

And then the door opens.

The fire is swallowed up in my body.

I step through the door.

The power is out and it's all dark except for the lightning making the sky bright reflecting through the corridors of the house. I feel my way along the walls—bumping into dressers and end tables, only able to see when the lightning splits the sky wide open.

Blackness is followed by the strobe of lightning and

then blackness and then lightning and then blackness. Thunder follows the lightning. The thunder makes the floorboards shudder beneath my feet. And then there is more blackness. And then lightning. And then blackness.

I reach the corner of the hall where I turn and feel my way down toward the front door. The rain is like a war being fought on all sides. The wind is like the howling of wolves after a kill. The thunder sets my teeth chattering.

The lightning strikes.

I see the silhouette of a crouched figure moving.

It is far away, down the end of the hall.

In the drowning blackness I call out, "Hello?"

Thunder takes the words from me.

I walk slowly toward what I cannot see.

And like a camera flashbulb popping, the hallway ignites with a lightning strike. And then I see my dad's face. His eyes are wide open and darting in every direction. Blood, dark and syrupy, is streaked across his mouth and dripping down his chin. He brings his arm up, his hand holding a knife with a long, curved blade covered in more black blood.

Then there is the dark.

It comes rushing in around me.

The thunder wrenches a sob from me as I startle and gasp for breath.

I hear the heavy blows and my father speaking in a whisper—very fast, like he's speaking in tongues.

I wait.

The lightning ignites the sky.

Bleeding out on the hardwood floor, Sheriff Jarrett lies unconscious, his eyes rolled back so only the whites are showing, his mouth gaping. My dad buries the knife deep in his chest.

I can't hold my scream back.

My dad's eyes fix on me and he removes the knife again and begins to stand. I turn and run as fast as I can, my lungs straining for breath. I hit a table and go down but then am up again and running faster— my way lit only by the lightning. I don't stop. I reach the stairs and run up them, sprinting, even as my legs burn and I can hardly breathe. My only plan is to get up to my room and then go down out the trellis—to climb down and escape into the woods. I can't think about anything else. I can't think about what happened. And yet I see Sheriff Jarrett's face as though frozen in my mind—projected forever on the backs of my eyelids. I cry and run.

I make it to the top floor and fall and slide along the carpet and then stumble to my room. Slamming and locking the door behind me, I sprint to the window. The rain and wind is so strong I can barely get it open. I push and struggle and pull and finally it opens just enough for me to fit through. Rain pours in through the open window as if I'd opened it underwater. I reach my hand around, feeling for the trellis on the side of the house.

But it isn't there.

I try again, sobbing and praying and running my hands along the rough, splintering wood. The trellis is gone. It must've fallen in the storm. I lean my head out and the rain is blowing sideways in the wind like shards of glass. It burns and pierces my skin.

"Fuck!" I yell out.

I know then that if I jump I will die.

I can't make it.

Struggling to get the window closed again, I sit down hard on the wet carpet and put my head in my hands and cry and cry.

It's over, I think.

There's no way out.

And I think maybe I should jump.

I mean, maybe I should just stop fighting. Maybe

jumping is peace. Maybe Christy knew the truth. Maybe the girl who lived here in Harmony House so long ago did, too.

But jumping isn't peace.

Peace is swallowing the rest of those pills and drifting off to sleep and never waking.

It seems to all make sense now.

Life is pain and hardship and like the myth of Sisyphus, that guy forever pushing the boulder up to the top of the hill only to have it roll all the way back down again.

Look at my dad: he grew up in this house, full of fear and superstition and self-hatred and unrequited love, and now he's a prisoner here—and I am, too. We will never get out. And it has to be that way.

He's right, in fact, the devil is in me and it was in my mom and it is in him, too—it is in this house. It is in the world. It is the only power there is. The lie is that there's the other power, the power of good and harmony and peace and understanding. We are all destined to be forever defeated, disappointed—to not get what we want—to be dashed against the rocks over and over and over again.

The lightning cracks and the thunder claps and I

walk to my closet and dig the bag of pills out of my jacket lining. I pour them out into my hand.

Is there enough here to kill me?

Jesus, I don't think there is.

I've taken too many of them already.

"Fuck!" I yell out loud.

I can't even kill myself right.

Unless maybe I take the pills and then go slit my wrists—or jump from the window or balcony.

The pills will take the pain of death away—and the pain of life, too.

I breathe in and out. The lightning turns the sky a sickly pale white. Thunder rattles the glass in the window. I hold the pills up shaking in my hand. And then Rose's words are there again like a nervous tic or a record skipping:

"I could teach you how to control the power you have," she said.

What the hell does that mean?

I have these visions.

I opened that door.

Did I do the other things, too?

Did I make that picture frame break over Alex's head?

Did I make Todd fall down the stairs?

Did I bring Colin back?

Did I cause that earthquake?

Did I cause this storm?

But none of that makes any sense.

If I had that kind of power I wouldn't be here. Sheriff Jarrett wouldn't be dead. Christy wouldn't have broken both her legs. I wouldn't be fucking pregnant.

I wouldn't've failed at every goddamn thing.

The thoughts come so fast it's like the pressure will explode my head wide open.

The fire in my insides ignites like gasoline through my veins.

If there's a power in me, then I need to use it now. I need to stop anyone else from getting hurt. And I need to bring this house crashing to the ground.

I look down at the pills in my hand.

Then I go to the window and push it open so the rain rages in.

"Fuck it," I say quietly.

I can't run anymore. Whatever's in me, I have to face it.

Now.

The way my mom never could.

I grip the pills and say a silent prayer.

I throw the pills out into the rain.

They disappear immediately.

Gone.

I try to breathe.

But I've made the decision.

I can live without them.

I can live.

Staring out into the rain, I blink, my eyes seeing the night turn back into a night long ago. Disoriented, I slump against the wall, watching the boy Anselm as he watches Sister Margaret again. Sister Angelica stands above her while she cries, holding her hands to her face. Anselm crouches behind a dresser, peering out from behind the corner. Sister Angelica bares her teeth and yells.

"You are a sinner. You must repent."

Sister Margaret cries and tells her, "Yes, yes, I want to repent."

And then Sister Angelica turns and sees the monsignor coming down the hall toward them. He grabs Sister Margaret by the arm and tells Sister Angelica, "Leave us."

Sister Angelica does as she's told.

Father Meyers drags Sister Margaret by the wrist into the bathroom. Anselm hears the water running in the

tub—loud—the pipes banging and sputtering. And then,
above the water and the pipes, comes the shrillest, piercing
scream. The sound echoes through the house. She screams
and then screams again.

The boy Anselm falls to his knees.

He covers his ears with his hands.

His mouth hangs open in a silent scream.

While Sister Margaret keeps on screaming.

And Anselm closes his eyes.

And it all goes black around him.

And then in the present I hear his body slam into the
door of my room.

The knob turns and the lock gives.

The door opens and the lightning strikes and my
dad holds up the silver cross and rosary, shouting, "I
adjure you, ancient serpent, by the judge of the living
and the dead, by your Creator, by the Creator of the
whole universe, by Him who has the power to con-
sign you to hell, to depart forthwith in fear, along with
your savage minions, from this servant of God, Jennifer
Noonan, who seeks refuge in the fold of the Church."

"Stop it!" I yell. "Stop it!"

I try to focus on my power. I try to take the flame in

me and direct it toward him. But he moves fast across the room—so fast it's as if he is disappearing and then reappearing again, closer and closer, 'til he is upon me.

He places the cross, burning, against my forehead and chants in a language that must be Latin but I've never heard him speak before.

"Imperat tibi Deus Pater; imperat tibi Deus Filius; imperat tibi Deus Spiritus Sanctus. Imperat tibi majestas Christi, aeternum Dei Verbum caro factum, qui pro salute generis nostri tua invidia perditi, humiliavit semetipsum factus obediens usque ad mortem; qui Ecclesiam suam aedificavit supra firmam petram, et portas inferi adversus eam numquam esse praevalituras edixit, cum ea ipse permansurus omnibus diebus usque ad consummationem saeculi."

The silver of the cross is like a knife blade cutting through the soft flesh on my cheek and I howl with the pain and the storm surges and the rain blows in sideways across the room.

My dad lifts me then, effortlessly, and carries me out into the hall and then down to the upstairs bathroom, where the water in the tub runs to overflowing.

As I close and open my eyes, the water turns to thick, coagulated blood and I see a vision of Sister Margaret drowned and bleeding below the surface. But then she is gone again and I'm being lowered into the frigid water.

My dad speaks with his eyes rolled back. "Vade satana, inventor et magister omnis fallaciae, hostis humanae salutis. Da locum Christo, in quo nihil invenisti de operibus tuis; da locum Ecclesiae Unae, Sanctae, Catholicae, et Apostolicae, quam Christus ipse acquisivit sanguine suo. Humiliare sub potenti manu Dei; contremisce et effuge, invocato a nobis sancto et terribili nomine Jesu, quem inferi tremunt, cui Virtutes caelorum et Potestates et Dominationes subjectae sunt, quem Cherubim et Seraphim indefessis vocibus laudant, dicentes: Sanctus, Sanctus, Sanctus Dominus Deus Sabaoth."

He forces my head under and I gasp and sputter and my lungs fill with water and I'm choking and the world is fading out.

I struggle and cough and get free for a minute, only to be plunged back down.

Under the water I open my eyes.

Through my open eyes I see my father's twisted, lunatic face—his teeth clenched, his eyes wild and blind to all reality. His sickness has turned him into a shadow of a person. His guilt has flayed the meat from his bones. His mind has warped like a wax figure left to melt in the sun. He has been destroyed by this house, by the church, by his humanity in the face of impossible expectations.

I grab hold of either side of the tub then and pull myself up. I breathe with needles in my lungs.

"Stop it!" I yell again. "Dad, please, you don't have to do this."

"The glory of the Lord is risen upon you!" he shouts. "I cast you out!"

He tries to push me down again, but I shake myself free.

"It wasn't your fault," I yell. "What happened to Sister Margaret—you didn't know what he was going to do to her. You didn't know he was going to kill her."

Hearing my words, my dad falls to his knees at the side of the tub. His eyes fill with blood and he cries with tears of blood streaming down his face.

"Silence, evil spirit," he shouts. "You will not trick me. I will not listen."

"Dad, it's the truth," I tell him.

He raises up then and he gnashes his teeth together and he shouts with a terrible high-pitched cracking to his voice, "I cast you out, devil!"

And then he puts one hand on my stomach and one hand on my head and I plead with him, "Dad, no. You don't have to . . ."

But he will not hear me. He presses his weight down on me and my head goes under again and water fills my mouth and he holds me there with the strength of ten men. I cannot move. I cannot even struggle. And I know if I swallow this water I will die.

I close my eyes.

I remember Rose's words.

I remember everything—every moment of my life—it plays like a sped-up film reel running through a projector. I see it all unfolding to this moment.

Not only that, but I see my father's life.

And my mother's, too.

I see the history of Harmony House passing before me in half a second.

And then I focus on the spark of hope—of flame—of smoldering fire at the base of my spine. I focus on it spreading from vertebra to vertebra—engulfing me—transforming my body into a pyre of burning embers.

Around me the water begins to steam and come quickly to a boil. My father yelps and withdraws his scalded hands. But I let the fire burn in me 'til the water is at a rolling boil and the shower curtains erupt in flame and the fire climbs the walls and the mirror shatters and the windows combust in a fireball of raining glass.

A noise tears through the house louder than anything that has come before—a terrible wrenching sound, like wood and metal being pulled slowly away from its foundation.

And then I hear my mother's voice.

She whispers softly to me.

I can't make out the words.

But they comfort me.

And soon the fire dies out.

And I curl onto my side.

Everything goes black around me.

And my mother's voice whispers.

Two perfect words.

"Thank you."

And then it all fades out.

CHAPTER 18

I open my eyes.

And I am in Harmony House.

The rain and wind has stopped.

I sit up and look.

A tree branch lies splayed across the bathroom—having broken through the side window and drywall. It's the twisted branch of an oak tree. And my dad is lying prostrate, crushed beneath it. He is dead. His mouth is open and his tongue is lolling. Blood pools beneath him.

Then I look down at myself—the blood dried and caked on my jeans. My stomach aches.

My father is dead.

And I must've miscarried.

The sun shines brightly now through the break in the wall. The smell of wet grass and rotted leaves and mud is thick in the air. I lean on the sink, then make my way over to my dad's crumpled body.

Stepping out into the hall I see that the roof has been torn off and the sky is blue and clear. The side of the house facing the street, too, has collapsed completely, so walking down the hallway is like walking in a giant doll's house.

I go to the room that was mine, the horrible pink walls stripped away. I grab a bag from under the bed and throw some clothes in it. I take off my blood-soaked jeans, too, and put on a pair of corduroys.

I hoist my bag up on my shoulder, climbing carefully down the collapsed stairwell, walking around Sheriff Jarrett's sprawled, dead body and stepping out of Harmony House for the last time.

Parked on the gravel, the sheriff's truck has been split almost completely in half by a fallen tree.

In fact, all the surrounding trees have fallen in the

storm. They lie like so many dead bodies, rotting, piled on top of one another.

Only the white oak remains standing—the one Sister Margaret carved her initials into—but with those two other letters—the ones I never saw in my vision.

AMJG.

I walk on down the driveway, climbing over fallen branches.

When I reach the street heading into town, I put my bag down and concentrate.

"I need a ride," I think. "I need a ride."

And then an old man in a pickup pulls to the curb.

"Some storm," he says as I open the passenger door.

"Sure was," I say.

"Where you headed?" he asks.

I don't answer him.

But he drives me to the Staffordshire Township Hospital—because that's where I want to go.

The hospital is overflowing with people injured from the storm, but I manage to find Christy's room on the third floor.

I duck my head in, carefully, trying not to make any noise opening the door. Christy is lying in the bed, her legs propped up in a cast, an old black-and-white movie playing on the wall-mounted TV. I recognize Robert Mitchum dressed as a preacher—right hand tattooed with "love," left hand tattooed with "hate." *The Night of the Hunter.* Christy watches absently. She seems okay. That, at least, is a relief.

Then from behind me I hear Rose's voice.

"You did it," she says. "Oh, Jen, I'm so proud of you."

I turn to her with my head bowed.

"Sheriff Jarrett came to the house last night," I say, feeling the tears at the backs of my eyes again. "My dad . . ."

"Shh," she says, not letting me finish. "Shh. I know. It's not your fault."

"But I could've saved him," I tell her.

She puts her big arms around me.

"You did everything you could."

She holds me to her. I smell the smell of her shampoo and laundry detergent. I start to cry.

"You don't have to worry anymore," she says. "You're safe now."

"I've got nowhere to go," I tell her.

She pushes my hair back out of my eyes.

"You'll stay with me," she says. "I'll protect you."

"But what do I do with this power I have?" I ask her.

"I don't know how to control it."

"You do know how," she says, smiling. "And I'll help teach you."

From her hospital bed, I hear Christy murmur weakly, "Jen? Is that you?"

"Yes," I say.

And I go to her.

"You'll stay with us now, won't you?"

I take her good hand in mine and feel the softness of her skin.

"Is that all right with you?" I ask.

She manages a smile.

"Yes," she says. "I want you to."

"Thank you," I tell her.

And then I turn away so she doesn't see me cry.

Rose walks over and takes me by the arm.

"Come on," she says. "I'll take you home."

"Home?" I ask.

"To my home," she says.

She smiles more.

I remember my mother's last words to me—in Harmony House.

"Thank you," she said.

And that's what I say now.

"Thank you," I tell Rose.

"It's all right," she says. "It's all going to be okay."

And for the first time since I can remember, I think that might be the truth.

I say good-bye to Christy, and then Rose and I walk out of the hospital together into the bright perfect clear cold sky.

HARMONY HOUSE
May 1961

Anselm Noonan
11 years old

EPILOGUE

It is a warm night—the moon half-full, shining bright across the grass. The leaves on the branches of the trees shimmer in the light. A cool breeze blows in from the ocean.

I climb out the open window and down the trellis on the side of the house that is overgrown with vines and purple blooming wisteria. I repeat a prayer to myself, saying it quietly over and over.

"God," I say. "I humbly offer myself to thee, to do with me and build with me as thou wilt. Thy will, not mine, be done."

I pray unceasingly—walking through the grass—smelling the damp earth—hearing the night sounds of mice and garden snakes and mosquitos. My linen dress shirt is damp with sweat down the back. My hand grasps at a small pocketknife. I say the prayer.

Any time I might have a thought about anything—anything sad or scary or mean or sinful—I just replace it with the thoughts of the prayer. I don't let myself think anything else. With the prayer, I am able to hold only God in my mind. And he makes me a channel of His will. And so I enact His will. I do nothing on my own. I do everything with God. And as long as I keep on praying to him, then nothing I do can ever be wrong.

So what happened to Sister Margaret, that was not my fault. It was God's will. His will guides me forward. His will, not mine, is being done.

Sister Margaret had to be punished.

Father Meyers was right.

For he is a man of God.

And I must follow him.

Just as I must follow Him.

"God, I humbly offer myself to thee. . . ."

I say it again.

I say it and say it.

I cannot stop.

I will never stop.

God's will makes me walk through the grass here and into the forest. His direction guides me to the tree—the great white oak—where Sister Margaret carved her initials with that boy—where she sinned against God. Now God has vested me with the power to make it right. He tells me what to do. He tells me to take the knife and with its blade to carve into the bark of the tree. On one side of the initials he has me put a G—a G for "God"—so that Sister Margaret can be with God, in the afterlife, for all time.

And then my hand moves to the other side, next to the initial M—next to Sister Margaret's initial—and I carve an A—bigger than the other letters—so that I can be with her forever more. Anselm and Margaret.

And God.

All together.

Forever more.

The power of God courses through me. It leaves me breathless and flushed with heat. The power of God is so strong it can raise me off the ground. I feel it all in my body. I feel it like a thousand electrical currents. I feel it in the very center of me. I feel it shiver for a long time—and then release.

Anselm and Margaret.

And God.

Together in Harmony House.

Never to part.

ACKNOWLEDGMENTS

Thank you: Amanda Urban, Kristen Pettit, Hrishi Desai, Molly Atlas, Dan Halsted, Nathan Miller, Ron Bernstein, Jeremy Kleiner, Felix Van Groeningen, Luke Davies, Brad Weston, Andre and Maria Jacquemetton, Patricia Resnick, Julia Cox, Nicole Yorkin, Tim Shaheen, Veena Sud, Peggy Knickerbocker, Armistead Maupin, Chris Turner, Gary Lennon, Jerry Stahl, Susan Andrews, Sue and Nan, Yoko and Sean.

And then my family: Jette Newell Sheff, papa and mama K, Jasper & Daisy, Mom, Nancy and Don, Susan and Steven, Mark and Jenny, Lucy, Becca, Bear, Joanie and Sumner. Is it dumb to thank dogs? They don't speak much human. But Ramona, Rhett, Cold War Charlie, and Cole, who's a very bad cat. Deep in my heart there's a house that can hold just about all of you.